Fresh Starts

&

Small Town

Hearts

KC Hart

Ebook

ISBN: 978-1-954791-16-9

Paperback

ISBN: 978-1-954791-17-6

For Em
You've encouraged me and guided me since day one. I never would have had the courage to try without you. Love you big.

BOOKS BY KC HART

A Christmas Blaze

Fresh Starts and Small Town Hearts

Business Smarts and Reckless Hearts

Car Smarts and Bashful Hearts

People Smarts and Wounded Hearts

Kid Smarts and Wistful Hearts

Family Smarts and Runaway Hearts

Elsie: Prairie Roses Collection

Moonlight, Murder and Small Town Secrets

Music, Murder and Small Town Romance

Memories. Murder and Small Town Money

Merry Murder and Small Town Santas

Medicine Murder and Small Town Scandal

Marriage, Murder & Small Town Schemes

Mistaken Murder & Small Town Status

Mistletoe, Murder & Small Town Scoundrels

Join KC's newsletter and receive a free ebook of Music Smarts and
Humble Hearts

PRAISE FOR KC HART BOOKS

A Christmas Blaze

A Pure Delight... *"This is one of the sweetest stories I've read! From tragedy to triumph, it draws you into the lives of each character. Don't miss this one!"*

Moonlight, Murder, & Small Town Secrets

"K.C. Hart knows how to grab your attention and keep you guessing."

"KC Hart tells the story with humor, wit, and the polite southern charm lacking in today's world. Keep an eye on KC Hart-she's good."...Author Richard M Wright

Music, Murder, & Small Town Romance

"If you loved Nancy Drew as a kid, you need to meet K.C. Hart!"

"A simple band competition turns into murder involving the local Casanova. This keeps you moving from one suspect to another without giving away the true villain. The dependence on God of the main character flows through the storyline in a very authentic way."

Memories, Murder, & Small Town Money

"I think this might be the best book in the series so far. The mystery is great, as usual, and kept me guessing until the end. I also really enjoyed seeing Katy's character grow and watch the sweet, honest friendship between her and Misty reach a new level. I highly recommend this book and the entire series."

"This is the most awesome series I've come across yet! I have been looking for a good Christian cozy mystery series and this is exactly what I have been searching for."

Merry Murder & Small Town Santas

"A great murder mystery that will pull you in from the beginning. So fun trying to figure out who is the killer. The author keeps the reader on a rollercoaster ride with clues and suspects. The town and characters are great fun and a little quirky. Katy is bold and gets herself into some situations that make her an excellent main character. I love reading this series and I'm looking forward to the next book. This is a clean book that doesn't have gore, but mystery and humor a plenty!"

"I loved this story, it was different. I never once gave the ending a thought, so it was a complete surprise. I love surprises! As always, the love between Katy and John was great, and the spiritual aspects were good also. The humor is always much appreciated."

Medicine, Murder & Small Town Scandal

"KC Hart gives hands and feet to a Christian way of life. KC Hart did it again. I love how her characters connect to my actual daily life. (Poor Katy, the struggle between chocolate pie and cholesterol!) I also love the way KC Hart makes belief in Jesus Christ an every day, every hour, every minute way of life, not something pulled out and shown off on "church" days or holidays.

If you need some down time, something to grab your attention and lose yourself for a few hours, get a KC Hart cozy mystery."

"Lots of twists and turns, and I had no clue "who done it" 'til the end! Loved the medical aspect too. Katy Cross keeps it interesting."

Marriage, Murder & Small Town Schemes

"You will get engulfed in this awesome Christian cozy mystery by the very talented author, KC Hart. I loved it and would highly recommend this book and the entire series."

"KC Hart doesn't disappoint with this one. This may be my new favorite!"

"I love the fact that this book has the same well developed, likable characters, along with a few new interesting ones added in... This is definitely a must read."

Mistaken Murder & Small Town Status

"Wow! Such an awesome book! I absolutely love that Christ is shared in Mistaken Murder & Small Town Status. This book kept me guessing until the very end. A definite must read. This is a great book to 'shoot the bull' about."

"Mistaken Murder & Small Town Status is a wonderful read. KC Hart has done it again with book seven of the Katy Cross Cozy Mystery series. Katy finds herself in the midst of another murder. This time it is a prize bull and the accidental death of a rancher... or was it really an accident? As the well developed plot progresses, the mystery thickens. I love how God takes a central part throughout the book. If you enjoy suspense and surprises, this is a must read."

Mistletoe, Murder &Small Town Scoundrels

"Katy Cross delivers once again! She wove family life, small town ties, and finding God's purpose into a page turner and this one kept me guessing to the end."

CHAPTER ONE

"*O*h, man." Vivian's hands fumbled through her designer bag, past the lipstick, perfume, year old Starbucks receipts, and other necessities one more time, but the house keys simply weren't there. "Think, Viv. Where did you leave them?"

Vivian Bradford rolled her lips in, biting down, her mind rapidly retracing her steps since she last had the keys to the historic home. She stared through the windshield of her sharp little red sports car, her brow furrowed, not seeing the electric blue morning glories in full bloom on the picket fence in front of the old home, the sprawling oak tree in the yard with the tire swing hanging down, and a blue jay perched in its center.

She arrived in Carson's Bayou late yesterday evening after driving nonstop for eight hours and checked into the only hotel in town. It had been too late to see the house then, but she grabbed dinner from a local place called the Gumbo Hut, and looked over the paperwork one more time. She still was having trouble wrapping her head around the fact that her grandmother left everything she owned to her.

When Vivian was a little girl, before her world had fallen apart, her parents would go on a getaway. They would drop her off every summer to spend a week with Cecille Bradford, Maw Cil, as she knew her. But that all changed when she was ten. Her father, Robert Bradford, had been convicted of money laundering and several other things that only the underbelly of society would do. Maw Cil's only son was shipped off to prison, and Vivian's connection with her grandmother and Carson's Bayou, was permanently severed.

Or so it had seemed.

Last month, when Vivian received a letter informing her of her grandmother's death, she was shocked to find she was the heir to the family home and a fairly substantial nest egg. The only stipulation had been that she would keep the home in good repair and would not sell it.

Vivian stepped from her little car onto the sidewalk, a blast of muggy heat hitting her in the face. Beads of sweat seemed to appear on her forehead and upper lip almost instantly. This incessant humidity was sure to ruin her makeup. The house keys had to be in her suitcase or the jacket she was wearing yesterday, both still back in her hotel room. She fanned her hand in front of her face deciding what to do. She didn't want to take the time to drive back across town to get the keys. By the time she searched her room and found the keys and drove back, the morning would be gone. Vivian groaned at the thought of wasting away that much of the day.

No, there was no need for that. If there was one thing Vivian Bradford knew how to do, it was how to break into a locked house. She was not a criminal. Not like her father, but for a couple of years after Robert Bradford went to prison, things were extremely rough for Vivian and her mother. Every penny of their money had gone to pay for her father's lawyers.

In the end, after all the exorbitant legal fees, her mother was flat broke, and they still sent her father to prison. Vivian would always remember turning on the TV to watch cartoons that day after school and seeing her father on the evening news, the bailiff taking him away in handcuffs, her mother crying in the background.

After that, her mother had moved them around, dodging landlords when the rent was past due. They often waited until after midnight to sneak back to the rental house or apartment to break in and get their meager belongings after the owner had changed the locks.

A few months ago, when she graduated from law school and passed the bar, she vowed her life would be different. She would be a lawyer with integrity, nothing like the ones her mother had dealt with during her parent's divorce.

Now she was moving to a town where the name Bradford stood for something good. She would rely on her grandmother's reputation to help her build a solid law practice with respectable clientele, people different from her father. She was starting a new life and leaving all those terrible memories behind.

First, though, she had to get into that house. She unlatched the little picket fence and hurried up the walkway, her high-heeled sandals clicking against the concrete. She walked up the three steps and paused, taking in the shady, wrap-around front porch with the swing at one end and red and pink knockout roses blooming in beds along the front.

The house had a massive solid oak front door that was as sturdy as the enormous tree shading the front yard. Vivian jiggled the antique doorknob with hope, but the dead bolt above it secured the fact that she would not be using her credit card to slip the lock to gain entrance to her new home. During her childhood visits, Maw Cil told her about how she had grown up in the old home, saying it had been in their family for over one hundred years. Now it belonged to her. It wasn't breaking and entering if she owned the place, right?

Vivian tucked a strand of black hair behind her ear, weighing her options. She paced along the porch in front of the four floor to ceiling windows, two on either side of the door. Kneeling down in front of each window, she looked for a way into the house. Three were closed tight, like they hadn't been opened in years. The fourth, though, the one on the end of the porch shaded by the ancient oak tree, was open just a crack.

Vivian looked over her shoulder at the quiet street behind her. A beat-up old truck was parked in the yard nearby, but no one seemed to be around. Good. She didn't want a witness to what she was about to do.

She turned back to the window and popped out the screen, laying it on the floor by her feet. Her fingers worked under the slit at the bottom of the window, probably ruining her manicure. The muscles in her arms strained to lift the stubborn window as it fought against her, refusing to move.

Vivian let go and pulled in a deep breath. She rolled up the flimsy silk sleeves of her designer blouse and set her feet apart, squatting and lifting the window again, using her leg muscles. The window finally budged just enough for her to squeeze through the opening. She tossed her hair back over her shoulder as she bent, pushing her upper body through the window. "Well, that's great," she mumbled. A pearl button on her cream-colored blouse snagged on the sill, making a hairline rip in the fabric, as she slithered her shoulders and torso through the narrow hole. Her hips and backside refused to mold into a shape that would cooperate.

"I don't know if I should pull you out, or shove you in." A deep, gravelly voice floated through the window from the porch behind her.

The pounding in Vivian's chest filled her ears as she

stopped struggling to unwedge herself. "This is not what it looks like," she snapped, turning her head to the side, trying to see who had caught her in such a precarious state. Her hair hung limp across her face, strands sticking to her pale pink lipstick. She lifted an arm from the floor where she was bracing her upper body inside the bedroom to brush away the hair, but quickly returned it to the floor as she felt her feet slip, threatening to leave her dangling like a fish on a hook. She sputtered and tried to blow the hair off of her mouth, waiting for the man to... what, leave, call the police? She moved her feet on the porch outside, to get a better footing, but felt her sandal fall off in the process.

"Looks like your rear end is stuck in Maw Cil's bedroom window," the voice said in a matter-of-fact tone. "Hold on."

Vivian felt the man's arms brush against her shirt, easily lifting the window and relieving her behind from its trap. She fell forward onto the hardwood floor, landing like a sea lion flopping around on the beach in one of those educational documentaries she loved as a kid. Rolling over and slapping the hair out of her face, she assessed the damage to her person. A button was missing from the front of her blouse and she had lost a shoe. Trying to maintain some semblance of dignity, she lifted her chin as she slipped the strap of her one sandal back on her heel. Her hand reached over and grabbed the windowsill, slowly pushing herself to her feet. She tugged her shirt into place before lifting her eyes to take a look at her rescuer.

"I'm Vivian Brad..." The words faded on her lips as she took in the appearance of the man before her. The man may have been decent to look at if she could actually see him under the layers of mud and dirt caked on his face, arms, and hands, but she couldn't tell. His tee-shirt, gray and wrinkled, was also covered in mud and ripped in several places. Her eyes traveled from the top of his blond head, broad shoul-

5

ders, and muscular arms, downward to his filthy jeans and mud caked work boots. "I'm Vivian Bradford, Cecille Bradford's granddaughter, and this is my home."

The man's outstretched hand held her other shoe as he stared at her with a rather smug smile on his lips.

"Thank you," Vivian sputtered, taking the sandal. "If you'll excuse me for a minute, I will be right out."

The man's eyes twinkled with amusement as he pulled his hand back through the opening and grabbed the window, pushing it shut. Vivian spun around, almost losing her balance on her one sandaled foot, but recovered quickly and stepped to the side, out of the man's line of vision to slip the other shoe back on. *Welcome to Carson's Bayou, Viv. Maw Cil would be so proud.*

CHAPTER TWO

*I*t was hotter than blue blazes, even in the cool mud under the ancient wooden house. Lucas listened as Mrs. Albertson chattered away from where she stood in her yard, waiting for him to crawl back out.

"Goodness, son, I didn't mean for you to get plumb filthy." Mrs. Albertson watched as Lucas slid on his belly back out from under the low-lying opening under the rear of her house. "I honestly didn't know who else to call, though. If you hadn't gotten those puppies out from under there, they probably would have starved slap to death."

Lucas crawled on his belly the rest of the way out from under the old house and looked at the three fat puppies sniffing around the elderly woman's ankles. They didn't look like they would be starving any time soon. "I'll cover that opening up so they can't get back under there, or you will be in the same predicament tonight with them whining, trying to find their way out." He stood up, running his fingers through his blond hair, which was now reddish brown with dirt from under the old woman's house. "I wonder where their momma is. I haven't seen a stray dog around, and it doesn't seem like they've missed any meals."

Mrs. Albertson looked down beside her walker, where one of the puppies was licking her black diabetic shoe. "I spilled a little milk this morning when I was fixing my oatmeal. I believe I must have gotten a little on my foot. Help me put these babies in the clothes basket on the front porch before you do anything else, son."

Lucas scooped up the three plump, wrinkly puppies in his arms and walked to the front porch, depositing them in a plastic clothes basket with tall sides so they couldn't escape. He walked back around to the side of the house where Mrs. Albertson was slowly picking her way through the yard, pushing her walker through the neatly cut grass. They both watched as a tiny red sports car drove past and pulled into the drive at the Bradford house down the street.

"You recognize that car?" Mrs. Albertson asked, craning her neck, trying to see who was behind the wheel.

"No, ma'am, I don't think I do." Lucas grabbed his hammer and a piece of the lumber laying nearby. He had brought boards with him to close up the open area in Mrs. Albertsons skirting around her house. "Do you need me to try to find those puppies a home? I don't want them to get under your feet and trip you up."

"No, that's alright. My grandson is coming by after he gets out of school. I'll get him to do that. You've done more than enough crawling through the mud under my house to drag them out." The wrinkles around her eyes deepened as she chuckled. "You're so caked with dirt that all I see is your eyes and teeth. You sure I can't give you a couple of dollars for your troubles?"

"Absolutely not." Lucas's eyes traveled down his muddy shirt and jeans. "But next time you make a batch of peanut butter cookies, give me a call, and we'll call it even."

"That dirt you are covered in is about the color of peanut butter."

"I know," Lucas winked at Mrs. Albertson, and his mouth stretched into a toothy smile. "That's what made me think of them."

Mrs. Albertson laughed as she turned and continued her slow, steady trek toward her porch. Lucas combed his fingers through his hair, sending a dust cloud up all around him like Pigpen from the "Peanuts" cartoon. He made a mental note to check back with his eighty-year-old neighbor that afternoon. He needed to make sure her teenage grandson did as she expected. The old woman loved dogs almost as much as she loved her grandchildren. She would have the puppies inside her house trying to bathe and care for them if someone didn't take them to a new home. With her poor balance, and the puppies' tendency to walk around her ankles and feet, she would end up with a broken hip by nightfall if he left them in her care.

Several minutes later, Mrs. Albertson was sitting in her rocker on the front porch, and the puppies were napping in the basket after being fed a bowl of milk. Lucas walked up the sidewalk past another house to his ranch style home on the corner lot. He stopped and opened his mailbox when a movement across the street caught his eye. The little sports car was still parked at Maw Cil's house, and it looked like whoever was over there was climbing in the bedroom window. He shoved the junk mail back in the box and trotted across the street, more curious than concerned. Any burglar worth their salt wouldn't try to break into the old house through the front window with all the elderly neighbors living around who were probably already dialing 911.

Lucas's eyes twinkled with amusement as he walked onto the top step of Maw Cil's front porch. A woman's head of shiny black hair disappeared through the bedroom window, followed by her narrow shoulders. Her curvy backside and long legs clad in form-fitting black jeans; however, remained on the outside of the window, obviously not able to fit through the opening. Lucas held in a chuckle as the woman's sandals slipped around on the porch floor. She was trying to gain traction without success. He took a cautious step closer, watching as one of the woman's legs slipped backwards, causing her sandal to fly off. His left hand shot out, instinctively catching the shoe, preventing it from smacking him in the head, while the woman's behind bobbed up higher in the air.

He listened for a moment as the woman grumbled about something from the other side of the window. "I don't know if I should pull you out or shove you in," he said, not really knowing for sure what to do in the situation. He didn't make a habit of grabbing strange women by the hips, and he wasn't too sure about how the woman would react, but it probably wouldn't be pleasant.

The woman's voice drifted across from the other side of the window, but it was obvious from the way her backside was wedged in the hole that she was not going any further through the narrow opening without a little help. He pulled in a deep breath and stepped closer. "It looks like your rear end is stuck in Maw Cil's bedroom window," he said, trying to figure out where to grab her to shove her through without being ungentlemanly.

He swallowed, pushing down the lump in his throat, and stepped behind her, leaning forward to grab the windowsill, trying not to get any closer to the woman's derriere than necessary. "Hold on."

The window raised easy enough, and the woman's bottom half slid through like a slinky, recoiling after a good stretch.

He watched the woman stand, her black hair flying around her as she rose from the floor, her cheeks hot pink with indignation. Even though he could hear perfectly well what she was saying, for some reason, he could not make his mind focus on the words coming from her lips. Heat crept up his neck, and he looked down at his hands to keep from staring at the woman on the other side of the window.

The shoe, I still have her shoe. He handed the sandal through the opening to the woman. His eyes transfixed as she nearly fell, hopping on one foot as she attempted to put the shoe back on. He swallowed hard and pulled his eyes away, sliding the window shut as she disappeared out of sight.

Vivian Bradford was back in Carson's Bayou, in her grandmother's house. She had not been back in fifteen years, but he would have recognized her face anywhere. They had played together when she came to visit her grandmother every summer as a kid, until suddenly, when he was twelve, the visits had stopped.

There had been some kind of scandal with her father that had landed him in prison. He had heard snatches of conversations from his parents about what happened, but since Robert Bradford only came to Carson's Bayou for a few days every summer, the topic was soon forgotten. But he did not forget a spunky little girl with the coal black hair and green eyes that would talk his head off. The corners of his lips slowly crept into a smile as he thought about all the times young Vivian had argued with the neighborhood kids. She made sure that when they played kickball in Maw Cil's backyard, the little kids got to kick as much as the big kids, even though she was usually the smallest one in the game.

If Vivian Bradford was moving into her grandmother's house, this might turn out to be an interesting summer.

CHAPTER THREE

*T*he antique metal doorknob was cool against Vivian's sweaty palm, even though everything else in the old house was sweltering from the heat trapped in by the closed windows. The place had been shut up tight since Maw Cil's death, and now the entire house was like an oven. She unlocked the heavy front door and yanked it open, letting a breath of fresh air and morning sunlight into the dark foyer. Her muddy rescuer turned from where he stood near the porch steps a few feet away. Did this man walk around in broad daylight this filthy all the time? Maybe he was homeless, or a hobo. Were hobos still a thing?

"Thank you for helping me." Vivian stepped through the doorway onto the porch, lifting a handful of thick black hair from her sweaty neck. "I actually own this house, so I wasn't trying to break in." She smiled politely at the man as his brown eyes continued to follow her every movement. "I seemed to have left my keys at the hotel where I am staying, and I didn't want to waste time driving back to get them."

Get a grip Viv. Why was she rambling to this filthy, quiet man? She didn't need to explain herself to him. "Let me grab my purse out of my car, and I will give you some money for helping me."

"Your front door needs to be rehung." The man stepped past Vivian to the old oak door open behind her. "See how it's scraping the floor here?" He pointed to the ancient dark varnish on the hardwood floors. A half-circle area, lighter than the rest of the floor, showed where the door had repeatedly rubbed against the wood every time it was opened, gradually scraping away the varnish. "I tried to get Maw Cil to let me fix it for her, but she kept putting me off. She always said she would get around to getting it done one day." He looked back up at Vivian and his face broke into a smile. "If you are planning on staying here tonight, you might want to go ahead and turn on the window unit in the bedroom before you leave. If not, you'll be roasted by in the morning."

Vivian's eyes roamed over the man's face. He obviously knew more about her grandmother's house than she did. "Thank you, Mr. uh?"

"Lucas," the man said. "No mister, just Lucas Wade. I live across the street." He nodded his head in the direction of the ranch house with the old truck parked out front. "Do you remember the old house that was there when you were a kid? It burned down twelve years ago. I wish my parents would have rebuilt it to match all the older houses in the neighborhood." He shrugged his shoulders. "But they wanted something more conventional for their retirement years."

Vivian looked across to the one-story, ranch-style brick house. It stuck out like a sore thumb among the older style homes up and down the street. The rest of the houses looked like her grandmother's. As she was driving up the street earlier, she noticed that most of the historic homes were restored to look like they belonged in a magazine. A few, however, had peeling paint, or sagging front porches, like they needed a good facelift.

Then there was this man's house across the street. His house didn't fit in the neighborhood at all. If they were in a large city, the homeowner's association would not have allowed the home to be built in a style that did not belong with the old world feel of the rest of the area.

Vivian turned her gaze from across the street, back to her grandmother's home. Now that she was taking a closer look, she could see that this house was needing some repairs as well. The grey-blue paint was peeling away in several places, the tin roof was blotched with brown rust stains, and it looked like the frame of one of the nearby windows was rotting away at the corners. She turned her eyes back to Lucas. "Well, I really do appreciate your help, and I will look into getting that door fixed." She glanced around, unsure what else the man was waiting for, then turned back to him, putting on a business smile. "As I said, my name is Vivian, and I will be happy to pay you for helping me through the window."

"No payment needed, except maybe a peach soda out of your refrigerator. It's warming up out here, Miss Bradford, and if I remember correctly, peach soda is your beverage of choice."

"You know who I am?" The corners of Vivian's eyes squinted together as she tried to see behind the dirt and mud hiding the man's face. "I don't think I've had a peach soda since the last time I was on this front porch. Maw Cil used to keep peach and orange and grape sodas for all the neighborhood kids."

"She still does, or did. If you don't mind, I'll step in and get us one."

"Uh... sure." Vivian followed her muddy rescuer's wide shoulders through the dark foyer into the adjoining room. Her eyes traveled upward to the twelve-foot ceiling, adjusting to the darker room, where a single light bulb hung from a chord in the center of the kitchen.

Lucas flipped a switch on the wall near the door frame, and the one-hundred-watt bulb lit up, revealing a refrigerator near the door that looked like it was made in the fifties. "I cleaned out everything in her refrigerator that would go bad before I locked the place up after the funeral," Lucas said, looking over his shoulder.

Memories flooded Vivian's thoughts as she recalled her grandmother cooking pancakes on the same old white stove she saw across the room. Her lips crept up in a smile as the memory of sitting at the little table with the metal legs and gold speckled Formica top drifted into her mind. The table still set there, shoved against the wall on the other side of the doorway. She stepped over and looked at one of the chairs with the green vinyl seat cover, cracked from years of use. Her eyes traveled back upward to where a dark water stain was visible on the ceiling in the corner. "I'm afraid my new home needs a little work." She turned and watched as Lucas took two little bottles of peach soda from the refrigerator and popped the tops on an antique bottle opener mounted to the white shiplap wall near the sink. "You seem to be quite at home in my grandmother's kitchen."

"I should be. I ate pecan pancakes with real butter, maple syrup, and sausage patties every Saturday morning right at that table from the time I was fifteen until she passed away last month." He handed one of the icy drinks across to Vivian and looked at the muddy fingerprints on the side of the bottle. "Excuse me a second," he said sheepishly. "I need to go wash up a little. I forgot how dirty I was."

Lucas hurried from the room and Vivian pulled a paper towel from a roll on a metal rack attached to the wall. The red brick floor, now covered with large muddy footprints in the shape of work boots, needed a good sweeping and mopping. She wiped the grime from her bottle and the one Lucas had left on the counter, before taking a long swallow of the drink.

The sweet soda burned her throat as it brought with it childhood memories of sitting on the back porch watching the older kids playing a game of kickball. She took a smaller sip as her thoughts traveled back to running through the sprinkler in her shorts and tee-shirt in the sweltering heat, screaming while Maw Cil plugged in the electric churn full of homemade banana ice cream.

Vivian wiped a bead of perspiration from her brow and sighed. She did not remember the place being this run down when she was visiting as a child, but her adult eyes could see that this old house needed a lot of work, much like some of the other ones on this street. Were those houses occupied by older people who couldn't afford to make the needed repairs on their fixed incomes?

Lucas had mentioned a window unit. If this house did not have central air conditioning, she would never survive in this southern heat and humidity. As a child, it had been a fun change to sleep in the little twin bed in one of the back bedrooms in front of a screened-in window. A box fan would whir all night long, mixing in with the sound of the crickets to lull her to sleep. Although it was a nice memory, she had no desire to repeat that scenario every night for the rest of the summer.

"I'll get this towel washed and bring it back over in a day or two."

Vivian's eyes blinked as she looked at the man standing in the doorway, a damp towel draped around his neck. His thick blond hair now lay to the side, damp above his tanned face and warm brown eyes. "I remember you," she said in surprise, studying his face. "You helped me learn to ride that old bicycle Maw Cil bought me at a garage sale one summer when I was little. You lived in the house across the street that looked exactly like this one."

"You were five, and I was seven." Lucas mopped his face with the corner of the towel and picked up the soda bottle from the kitchen counter. "I really hated it when our house burned. More than my parents did, I think." He held the cold drink bottle to his forehead. "You want to go back on the front porch where it's a little cooler? Even with these high ceilings, it is starting to get mighty warm in here with the windows closed."

Vivian followed Lucas back out front, leaving the front door open for now. She sat on the porch swing near the bedroom window where she had recently fallen through and watched as Lucas sat on the edge of the porch, letting his feet hang off the side near the rosebushes. "I guess you and Maw Cil were close if you two shared breakfast every Saturday."

"You could say that I am one of her many adopted grandchildren. I was always playing with the other kids in her backyard and coming over when I saw her working in her flower beds out front. When I was fifteen, I started mowing her grass in the summer and raking her leaves in the winter. I wouldn't take any money, so she paid me in pancakes, and knitted me a new beanie cap every year. I have a beanie in almost every color imaginable."

"I have a beanie in a box somewhere from when..." Vivian paused and pushed the corner of the swing with her toe. No need to dredge up why she had quit coming to see her grandmother. "From when I used to visit." She took another sip of her peach soda. "I guess I better lock the place back up. It appears this house needs a lot of work to get it modernized before I can live here."

"So, you are planning on moving in?" Lucas's brow furrowed. "You won't be selling Maw Cil's house?"

"No, I will be living here. I guess I need to find a

carpenter who can get the work done soon, since I'm starting my new job next week. I need to get someone to work on the house that I can trust, that I won't have to keep an eye on. I hope to be so busy at my practice that I won't have time to deal with house renovations."

"Well, I think I know the perfect man for the job." Lucas set the empty drink bottle down beside him and reached in his back jeans pocket. He pulled out his wallet, retrieved a business card, and stretched his arm up to Vivian. "I already know almost everything that needs to be done to your house, but I still need to go back over the place to make sure I give you a complete estimate. I tried to get Maw Cil to let me fix things up for years, but she wouldn't do it. I'm not sure why. I told her I would do it for only the price of the materials. Maybe that wounded her pride or maybe she didn't want to deal with it or maybe she didn't see all the problems. Either way, I know this house almost as well as I know my own."

Vivian took the card and read:

LUCAS WADE
Carpentry
Construction
General handyman

*S*he looked up and studied the man sitting at her feet. "I will need references." Vivian appreciated his offer, but if Lucas was still living with his parents, she was not sure he was the person she wanted doing the repairs to her home. She needed the home to not only be updated, but also made into a place where she could host parties for people she wanted to impress. Lucas Wade seemed to be a nice enough guy, but this was an important step in her plan of building a life with a solid reputation in Carson's Bayou. She couldn't risk letting her laid-back neighbor mess up her plans.

"Of course." Lucas nodded, not appearing offended by her statement at all. "I'm well known around here, so I can get you plenty of references. I finished building a spectacular house for Blaze Carson over on the old side of town near the fire station. I can get you a list of people that I have done renovations for on their older homes, as well."

"Alright." Vivian stood from the swing, her empty bottle in her hand. "I guess I better be on my way." She looked down at the phone number on the bottom of the business card. "I will be calling you within the next day or two if I decide to use you."

"Okay." Lucas stood and took the bottle from her hand. "I live right across the road, though. If you can't get me by phone, just come over any time. If my truck is in the drive-way, I'm home." He watched as she pulled the front door shut and locked it. "By the way, if you need to get back inside, there's a spare key under a rock in the flower bed. No need to go through the window again... unless, of course, you want to."

CHAPTER FOUR

*T*he following afternoon, Lucas got out of his truck and checked his mail before heading into his house.

Why did he give her his old card from back when he first started his business? He kept that thing in his wallet for nostalgic reasons. Why didn't he give her one of his "Wade Brothers Construction" business cards?

Who was he trying to kid? He knew exactly why he had given Vivian Bradford his old card. It had his personal cell on it instead of the office number for the company. If she happened to call the office, Mrs. Dean, the secretary, would put her in contact with Langston, Lucas's older brother. Langston handled the work contracts and paperwork end of the business, while he handled the hands-on building end.

He wasn't worried about his older brother talking to Vivian for any particular reason, except that Langston would expect Lucas to get an estimate of the job, then turn the actual work over to one of their crews. Langston enjoyed his role of wearing the suit, meeting the prospective customers in their office across town, and talking prices and contracts.

That; however, was not Lucas's thing. He had an office because Langston insisted. He had a suit because Langston insisted, but both things got little use. He preferred being out on the sites, working with the crews, and making sure the work was done correctly and no corners were being cut.

What Lucas loved the most, though, was actually building new houses or restoring the old homes. Being outside, laying the foundation, putting up the walls, the windows, the roof, he loved it all. When the families came by and stared at the property in whatever stage of completion the home was in, it always made him smile. He was helping give someone their dream. He didn't get that feeling in an office.

Lucas unlocked his front door and stepped inside. He glanced over his shoulder across the street to Maw Cil's house before shutting his door. Vivian's little red sports car was not there. He hung his cap on the hook in the little foyer and headed through the living room to the kitchen, not bothering with turning on the lights. He always left the curtains open, and the evening sun was still bright at six pm this time of year.

Lucas unbuttoned his tan Wade Brothers Construction work shirt as he walked through the house and tossed it on the back of a barstool in the kitchen. His plain white tee-shirt suited him better, but he understood why Langston wanted all the men to wear these shirts when they were on a job.

The jug of milk felt light as he pulled it from the refrigerator, almost empty. Time to make a grocery run. He would check and see what Mrs. Albertson wanted him to pick up for her from the store. He would grab some milk, oatmeal cookies, and a few other essentials, along with whatever his old neighbor needed. He looked at the mostly empty shelves of the refrigerator before shutting the door.

After talking with Vivian yesterday, he had gone to a

work site where one of his crews was building a two-story home for a couple who were moving back to Carson's Bayou to retire. That afternoon, when he got home, he visited Mrs. Albertson again. Her grandson had taken the puppies as she had expected, so that was one less thing for him to be concerned about today.

Yesterday ended with him sitting alone on his front porch listening to music on his phone until the mosquitos started attacking, hoping Vivian would come back by, but she had not. Even though he had been busy all day, his mind kept returning to his new neighbor across the street. She had looked so cute hopping on one foot inside of Maw Cil's bedroom yesterday after he gave her back her shoe.

His phone buzzed, pulling him away from his thoughts. He pulled it from his jeans pocket as he took the lid off the almost empty milk jug. Debating on getting a glass, he drank the few swallows straight from the container. "Hello." He glanced at the number on the screen but didn't recognize it.

"Lucas, this is Vivian Bradford from yesterday. I've made some inquiries about your work, and I need to apologize. I did not realize that you owned such a prestigious construction company. You did the restoration work on the mayor's home so it would meet the requirements for the historical register?"

"Yes, that was a couple of years ago." Lucas walked over to the bar and set the milk jug down. "That job took quite a while, but I think it turned out pretty nice."

"I should say so." Vivian's voice gushed through the phone. "I am looking at some pictures of the place from a feature on historical homes from Southern Life magazine. How soon can we meet to get you started on my house?"

"How about tonight? I have to pick up a few groceries, but I can grab a pizza and bring it over and look around. I should be able to give you a ballpark figure of the cost this evening. I can get an actual estimate to you before the end of the week."

"That sounds great. I will get something for dessert. See you in a bit."

"That's more than I was expecting." Vivian frowned at the dollar figure Lucas had written down on the piece of paper. "That will take every bit of the money my grandmother left me."

"I'm really surprised she was able to leave you any money at all when she passed away." Lucas picked a pepperoni circle from his pizza slice and popped it into his mouth. "She seemed to have fallen on hard times for the last several years."

"She had a very large life insurance policy that was most of the money, along with some funds she had in some IRA accounts." Vivian breathed in the smell of honeysuckle blooms coming from the picket fence along the edge of the spacious backyard. "I lost touch with her. I didn't know she was struggling."

"In the wintertime, Ma Cil used to close off the rest of the house and live in her little bedroom to save money on the heating bill. She would go to the kitchen on Saturdays when she made us pancakes and cook enough meals for her to live on for the rest of the week. She would heat dishes in the microwave or the hot plate she kept in her bedroom. There's basically zero insulation in this old house, and she couldn't afford to keep the entire place warm. She lived in her bedroom and kept a fire in the fireplace. Even with her oven on in the kitchen to use as a heater, we could see our breath some winter mornings when we were in there eating our breakfast."

"There's the leaky roof, the bad plumbing, and none of this ancient wiring is up to code." Lucas looked at the house behind him where he had spent so much of his childhood. "I'll have to climb under the house tomorrow to check the foundation, and also look around in the attic to make sure I haven't missed any other problems. It takes a lot to keep these old places going. She didn't want to move, but she couldn't afford to get the repairs done either. I would have helped her more if she would have let me, but she refused all my offers to make repairs. I did her yard work and brought her firewood, but that was pushing the limit of what she would accept. She had always been used to helping others. She did not enjoy being on the receiving end of charity."

"Oh, wow." Vivian's brow furrowed. "I had no idea it was that bad. I remember my grandmother always seemed to be well off. She drove that big Cadillac, and I remember her having people over in the summer for parties during my visits. Every summer she always took me to a shelter some-where in town to donate the beanies she knitted for them and the blankets the ladies at her church made. She said she wanted to teach me how important it was for the ones who were blessed with things to share with those in need. I always assumed she had plenty of money." Vivian tossed the end of a piece of pizza back into the open box sitting on the picnic table. She looked around the backyard where they were having dinner. "I guess my memory of how things seemed is a little different from how they actually were."

"No, not exactly." Lucas picked up his bottle of peach soda and took a swallow. "I don't know what all happened with your father before he, uh, well, before he went to prison." Lucas glanced over at Vivian, whose eyes had taken on a deer in the headlights look. "I believe your grandmother put a lot of money in your father's business, trying to keep him afloat and out of trouble."

Vivian wiped her fingers on a napkin and swatted at a mosquito that landed on her arm. "Well, thank you for the pizza, but I think I need to call it an evening. I have a busy day tomorrow."

"Look." Lucas's eyes searched Vivian's distressed face. "I'm sorry I brought up your father. It's none of my business, really." He stood from the picnic bench and began helping Vivian pick up their paper plates. "Don't you want to eat these fancy looking cupcakes you got us? If you will stay, I promise not to mention your... family anymore."

Vivian shoved the greasy paper plates and napkins in the black trash bag and looked down at the cupcakes she had picked up at a bakery near the law office where she would soon be starting work. Her shoulders sagged as the weight of her father's sins pushed down upon her.

"I'm not trying to be ungrateful. It's simply that I am desperately trying to leave all my father's drama behind me. I was hoping when I got the letter stating Maw Cil had left this place to me that God was giving me a second chance. I wanted to move here and just be Vivian Bradford, not the daughter of Robert Bradford, the crook that was connected to a bunch of thieves and drug dealers."

"And you can do that."

"No." Vivian pulled in a deep breath and dropped the trash bag at her feet. "No, I can't. Not if my father's tentacles were in my grandmother, destroying her reputation too."

"Vivian." Lucas stepped over to where Vivian leaned against the table, staring across the yard seeing her dreams disappearing before she had a chance to make them a reality. He placed a hand on her shoulder. "I don't know what you've heard about your grandmother from the people in this town, but there is one thing that is certain. No one blames Maw Cil for what happened with her son." He waited for her to look at him, but she kept staring straight ahead. "Nobody will blame you, either."

He continued to stand at her side for a few more minutes, but Vivian remained quiet. "I guess I better get back home." He reached down and picked up the trash bag from the ground and tossed his empty drink bottle in.

"Don't forget your cupcake." Vivian finally picked up the pastry box and held it out to Lucas.

Lucas looked through the dim setting sun at Vivian's tear-stained face. He wanted to tell her she was not alone, that he was in her corner. He wanted to wipe the tears off of her cheeks and brush the strands of coal black hair out of her eyes, but he didn't. "Thanks. I will call you when I have a written estimate."

"Okay." Vivian wiped her cheek with the back of her hand. "I'm going to figure out how to get this house fixed, and get what I want, Lucas. I'm not going to let my father stop me."

"I don't doubt that, Vivian... not at all."

CHAPTER FIVE

$\mathcal{V}$ ivian's fingernails drummed against the Formica tabletop in the outdated kitchen of her new home. She had to come up with a plan to get this house fixed up to be suitable for the type of lifestyle and status she needed to be a success. According to the will, she couldn't sell the place, nor did she want to. This house anchored her connection to her grandmother and to the people of Carson's Bayou.

The problem was, she had been running on financial fumes for the last two years. Her job had barely made enough to pay her part of the rent on the apartment she had shared with her roommate back in Georgia. She still had her car note, living expenses, and payments on all the student loans she had taken out to get her coveted law degree. Without her grandmother's inheritance, her bank account was a nightmare. She probably couldn't even get a bank to loan her the money to make up the small gap in what Maw Cil had left her and the amount she needed to fix the house.

Oh well, maybe something would come to her while she worked. Her goal for today was to get the stale air and dust out of the place and make it as livable as possible. She had checked out of the hotel that morning, so she was officially living in the musty, old house. She stepped over to the stainless steel double sink, dull with dust. A drip of water dropped from the faucet into the drain. Water, at least the water was turned on and working. That was another thing that hadn't crossed her mind. The lawyer who settled the will must have been paying the electricity and water bill out of the money her grandmother left her.

A smile softened Vivian's worried face as she looked out the kitchen window to the enormous orange tabby cat perched on the ledge. She reached across the sink and pushed the window up with a little effort. The cat scampered away, jumping to the shady ground below and disappearing under the picket fence into a neighbor's yard. A morning breeze blew in from the outside and felt good against her face. The first order of business would be to open all the windows... or break her back trying.

"There you are." Three hours later, Vivian sat on her front steps drinking a bottle of water. She watched as the orange tabby made its way across her front porch to where she sat. She mopped her forehead with the tail of her gray tank top and leaned back against the porch column behind her, the chips of flaking paint sticking to her sweaty shoulders. "You missed round one of the work, but I will sign you up for round two."

The tabby strolled down the steps and rubbed his furry back against Vivian's tanned leg. She reached down and scratched the cat behind his ears. "There's no collar. Are you a neighborhood traveler?" That was a term Maw Cil had called the stray cats and dogs that Vivian would find during her summer visits. She had often tried talking her grandmother into bringing a visiting cat or dog into her home and claiming it, but her grandmother always refused. "This animal is not used to staying in the same place or living indoors," Maw Cil explained, one summer morning when five-year-old Vivian had found a lanky, white tomcat on their front porch and claimed him for her own. "We'll give him a bite to eat during his visit, and I promise you, he will come back to see you again."

"Hello there." An old lady dressed in a faded housecoat snapped down the front, white support hose, and black diabetic shoes, slowly made her way up the sidewalk, pushing a walker with a basket connected to the front. "I saw your little red car come by this morning and decided to come introduce myself. I'm Ruthie Albertson. I live a couple of houses down." The old woman paused at Vivian's gate. "Do you mind if I come in? I see you've already met Truman."

"Of course you can come in." Vivian hopped up and trotted down her short walkway to open the gate in the middle of her picket fence. "Let me grab you a chair from inside so you won't have to climb my steps." Vivian hurried inside and picked up one of the old metal chairs with the green vinyl seat cushions. "I'm sorry this chair is in such awful shape," she said, lugging it down the stairs and setting it on the shady walkway. "I'm just getting started looking around inside, and I'm afraid I have a lot of work to do." The yellow tabby waited for Mrs. Albertson to settle herself in the chair, then hopped into her lap with a thud. "Is Truman yours? He sure is a big cat."

"He's mine and yours and everybody else's on this street." Mrs. Albertson rubbed the cat's back as it raised like a horseshoe to meet her hand. "I think he owns us, because we definitely don't own him."

"Can I get you something to drink?" Vivian breathed in the scent of morning glories and honeysuckle growing on her fence as she smiled down at Mrs. Albertson. "I have water and a few bottles of grape and orange soda in the fridge. I've finished off the peach."

"No, honey. I wanted to stop by and bring you some of my cookies to welcome you to the neighborhood." Mrs. Albertson tilted her head to the side and looked at Vivian. "I hope you aren't planning on selling Cil's house to some stranger."

"No, ma'am. I'm in the process of moving in." Vivian paused. "Do you know who I am?"

"I know you are Cil Bradford's granddaughter. I can't recall your name, though. You won't remember this, but your grandmother had the same thick black hair that you have, and you favor her way more than your daddy ever did. He looked more like your grandfather."

"I never met my grandfather. He died before I was born." Vivian raised the water bottle to her lips, emptying it of its final few drops as her eyes traveled across the front yard. "Were you and Maw Cil friends?"

"Everyone loved Cil, but yes, we were great friends. We went to school together, and when I got married, I was tickled pink that we were neighbors. I'm so glad you are moving into her place. It really broke her heart when she wasn't allowed to see you anymore."

"What do you mean?" Vivian's green eyes turned back to her visitor. "I thought she didn't want..." Vivian's voice grew fainter as she thought about what her neighbor said. She plastered on the smile she had learned to use from years of covering up the embarrassing situations she often found herself in as a child and teen. "I thought she decided to stop my summer visits because she was too busy or something."

"No, sweetheart." Mrs. Albertson reached her soft wrinkled hand over and patted Vivian's knee. "When that scandal happened to your daddy, your momma disappeared with you." Mrs. Albertson took a deep breath and shook her head. "Your grandmother thought your mother was afraid she would try to take you from her. Cil did everything in her power to find you two, but nothing ever came of it. I'm sure she's sitting up in heaven as pleased as pie that you are here now."

Vivian sat on the step and leaned her head back against the porch column remembering all the times they had run away from an angry landlord, floored by the revelation that her grandmother had not been the reason her visits had stopped. She had changed schools more times than she cared to count. How different her life might have been if her mother had not been so untrusting and had allowed Maw Cil to help them.

"Lucas tells me he's going to fix up your place." Mrs. Albertson sat back up and reached in the basket of her walker. "I tell you what, you won't find a better carpenter... or a better man in all of Carson's Bayou." She pulled a plastic container from the basket and passed it over to Vivian. "I made this batch of peanut butter cookies last night. I hope you enjoy them. They are Lucas's favorite." She looked down and tugged on the edge of her housecoat. "It's a shame what happened to that man. It's about time for him to meet a decent girl and get back to living."

"You are so nice. Thank you so much." Vivian took the container from Mrs. Albertson's hand and opened the sealed lid. She inhaled the cookie's tantalizing aroma and rolled her eyes upward. "I'm going to have one now, if you don't mind. I skipped breakfast." She stretched her arm out toward the old woman. "Want one?"

"I believe I will." Mrs. Albertson took a cookie from the container. "I like chocolate chip better. Lucas climbed under my house and rescued a few puppies for me the other day, so I made his favorite for him." She nibbled the edge of the cookie and looked at Vivian out of the corner of her eye. "If you see him today, tell him I have the cookies for him."

Truman's orange hairy body weaved between Vivian's legs, trying to see if he wanted to ask for some of what the black-haired woman was eating. "He's supposed to come over this afternoon to discuss the renovations with me," Vivian said, breaking a tiny piece of the cookie off and setting it between her feet for the cat to sample. "I'll tell him then. Your cookies are really good. I'm not a great baker. Are these hard to make?"

"Not at all. I'll get the recipe for you." Mrs. Albertson blotted a crumb from her chin. "You can get everything at the Sunflower over by the dollar store. It's a lot cheaper than that super center place on the new side of town. I'll have to get you to drive me around town in that fancy little red car one day soon and show you all the good places to shop."

"We can do that," Vivian said, grinning at her spunky neighbor. "I have to find a dentist, a doctor, and a hairdresser too."

"And you are more than welcome to pick me up for church Sunday." Mrs. Albertson paused and cleared her throat. "Are you a believer, honey?"

"Believer?"

"Yes, honey. Are you a Christian?"

"Yes, ma'am." The corners of Vivian's lips pushed up into a smile. "No one has asked me that question in a long, long time, probably since I was a kid. I gave Jesus my life when I was in college. I had been trying to deal with a lot of problems. I finally realized that I was a mess that only God could fix."

"Oh, aren't we all?" Mrs. Albertson shoved her large square glasses up on her nose. "Most people just don't know it. Well, if you haven't found a church home yet, why don't you come with me on Sunday? Like I said, we could even ride in your pretty red car."

Vivian's eyes twinkled at her new friend's boldness. "I believe I might actually take you up on that invitation."

After Mrs. Albertson left, Vivian toted the worn-out chair back to her kitchen. Lucas would be coming over after while, and she had to figure out a way to get the repairs done to her house. She set the container of cookies on the counter and looked around the kitchen. Hadn't he mentioned offering to do the repairs for his grandmother for the cost of the materials? She couldn't ask him to do that kind of thing for her any more than her grandmother could. How would it sound if word got out that she couldn't even pay her own bills? No, she would have to come up with something. She looked down at her cut off-blue jean shorts and flip-flops. She didn't look much like a lawyer today, but that's why her plan was so important. She needed to develop the image to go along with the job.

Vivian looked toward the doorway of the kitchen as a crashing sound came from the foyer. She had left the front door open, feeling completely safe on the quiet street, but who was coming into her home? She opened the fridge and pulled a sweaty bottle of grape soda out, holding it upside down by the neck. If needed, the bottle would do if she had to hit an attacker over the head.

"Oh, you. You scared the daylights out of me." Vivian stepped into the foyer and watched as Truman made his way down the hallway, acting like he owned the place. The broom she had left propped in the corner by the umbrella stand was now laying on the floor in the doorway. "Well, come on in and make yourself at home," she said to the orange cat. "If you have any ideas on how to renovate a rundown historic home on a shoestring budget, I'm all ears."

"I'm sure I can come up with something."

Vivian's hand flew to her chest, and her eyes darted to the doorway. A man wearing an expensive-looking suit and confident smile stepped over the broom and into her home. "You scared the daylights out of me." She lowered the drink bottle from over her head. "Can I help you?"

"I'm Finley Parson. You are coming to work at our firm next week. I'm just stopping in to make sure you are getting settled in to our little town."

CHAPTER SIX

*L*ater that day, Lucas sat on the steps of his porch and slipped on his tennis shoes, glad to be in a clean tee-shirt and jeans. After a sweaty day of working on one of several homes his company was building in a new subdivision across town, the shower and a change of clothes were exactly what he needed.

Maw Cil's house had been on his mind all day, but he believed he had come up with a plan to help Vivian get the renovations done. Instead of going through Wade Brothers Construction, he would do all the work himself as a side job. That way, he could give her an estimate that would fit her budget. The only problem was, he wasn't exactly sure what her budget was. He could cut his labor fees and shop around for suppliers on his own. Of course, he hadn't talked to his brother Langston about any of this. Langston would not be happy. His brother didn't mind him doing small repairs as side jobs for people as long as it didn't take money away from the company. This; however, could be an extremely lucrative contract if Vivian had the funds, but that was the problem. She didn't have the funds.

Lucas stood from his porch steps and ran his fingers through his hair, still damp from the shower. Would helping Vivian be taking money out of Wade Brothers pockets? That would be how Langston saw this. If he took this job from the company, he would be taking work from his employees, men who depended on their business for a paycheck. His eyebrows drew together as he looked across the street at the house where he had spent so many days.

The front door opened, and Vivian stepped out from inside the house as he started down his walkway and across the street. The white cotton sundress with eyelet lace made his new neighbor look cool and welcoming. Her black hair was pulled up away from her face, which was framed by a pair of large silver hoop earrings. Lucas was glad he had taken the time to get cleaned up, instead of wearing his dirty work clothes and muddy boots over like he had almost done in his hurry to see her.

"You sure do look nice." Lucas stopped at the bottom of her steps, a playful grin on his face. "I have to say that the view from my front porch has improved since you came to town."

An unexpected blush crept across Vivian's face, and she rubbed her pink lips together. "Thank you. It has been a very busy, and very interesting day." She reached up and touched a slim strand of black hair that slipped from the hair band and drifted near her cheek. "Do you want to come in and talk business? I've had the windows raised all day and found some box fans to put in a few of them, but it's still pretty warm everywhere except for my bedroom. I am following Maw Cil's example and have the little air conditioning unit going in there."

"Have you had dinner?" Lucas slipped his left hand in the front pocket of his jeans. "We could run over to the Gumbo Hut and grab a bite to eat first."

"That sounds perfect." Vivian's eyes traveled across the street to Lucas's old truck. "Do you mind if we go in my car? I, uh, don't want to risk getting my white dress dirty brushing up against your truck."

"Sure." Lucas looked over his shoulder to the old eighties model Ford. Langston had begged him for years to get another truck, but he had so many memories attached to his old pickup. He rubbed his hand along the back of his neck, pushing away thoughts he didn't want to deal with. He turned back to Vivian. "I guess I could give it a bath every couple of years or so."

"I don't know." A mischievous glint flashed in Vivian's eyes. "Dirt may be the only thing holding it together. You may not want to risk it."

"I guess it doesn't look like much, but the food here is top-notch." Lucas let his eyes roam around the restaurant before settling on Vivian. "You can probably tell that by how crowded the place is."

"Yes. That seems to be the case." Vivian picked up her glass of iced tea and stirred it with the plastic straw as she looked around the room.

Families, teenagers, couples, friends, all sat around her at the little tables with their vinyl tablecloths and wooden chairs, chatting and eating their food. There were no singles like she was used to seeing at the coffee shops she had frequented before her move, all sitting alone and most staring at a laptop or cell phone. She smiled at the waitress who stepped up and set a plate of crawfish pie in front of her.

Vivian raised an eyebrow as she looked over at the steamy

bowl of seafood gumbo the woman placed in front of Lucas. "I hope I like this."

"Taste it." Lucas pulled a paper napkin from the silver holder in the center of their little table. "If you don't, I will trade with you. I like everything on the menu." He watched as she dipped her fork through the crust of the meaty pie and brought a small bite to her lips.

Vivian's eyes stretched wide as she swallowed her food and stuck her fork back into the dish for a bigger bite. "No trading. Oh. My. Goodness. This is amazing."

"See." Lucas blew the curl of steam rising from his bowl. "They also do lunch deliveries. I have their number saved in my phone. I remodeled Aunt Delphine's house a few years ago, and now she always treats me right."

"You are related to the owner?"

"No. Aunt Delphine is not really my aunt. Everybody just calls her that. But if she knows an order is for me, she always puts something extra in my bag."

"So, what you are saying is that you are a man with connections." Vivian's eyes twinkled with amusement as she took another sip of her tea.

"Well." Lucas reached up and lifted the collar of his tee-shirt with both hands. "With great power comes great responsibilities, but if you play your cards right, I may be able to get you a couple of boudin balls for the road."

"Oh my, what a charmer."

Vivian's laughter floated across the table, and Lucas felt his pulse do a little flip. "Only for special people."

They continued their banter through the rest of the meal, and neither attempted to bring up the reason for their meeting until saucers of strawberry shortcake were set in front of them.

"I've been thinking about your renovations." Lucas cut his fork through the whipped cream, strawberries, and moist yellow cake. "I think I've come up with a solution so that you can get the remodeling done."

"About that." Vivian cleared her throat and laid her fork back on her plate. "One of the lawyers I will be working with came by the house today. Do you know Finley Parson?"

"Yeah. I know Fin." Lucas raised his fork to his lips, not tasting the cake as he looked at Vivian. Finley had been in his brother Langston's class throughout school, and the two had been roommates for a while in college. Finley was an alright guy, he guessed... for a lawyer.

"Well, he dropped by today while I was airing out the house to introduce himself, since we will be working together. I mentioned that I'm getting ready to start remodeling the house, and..." Vivian bit her lower lip and looked over Lucas's shoulder where someone had started a zydeco song about cornbread. "He went with me to First National. I'm sure you know that his father is the bank president there."

"Yes. He is."

Vivian picked up her tea glass and set it back down without taking a drink. "Finley explained the situation with Maw Cil's house, and the will, and me moving to town and everything to his father." Her eyes finally turned back to Lucas's face. "He was able to get the bank to give me the loan for the extra money I need to get the house finished the way I want to."

"Oh." Lucas set down his fork, his taste for strawberry shortcake suddenly gone. "That's great news. I will get Langston to get the paperwork together for you." He paused and leaned back in his chair. "As a matter of fact, why don't you go by the office tomorrow and make an appointment with him. He will work out all the details so a crew can get started on your place."

"That sounds great." Vivian's voice lost the playfulness it

had only a few minutes before. "When do you think you, I mean your crew, can get started?"

"Tell Langston you are my neighbor and I said to move you up to the top of the list." Lucas picked his napkin up from his lap and laid it on his saucer. "They should be able to start next week."

"Oh." Vivian watched Lucas as he signaled to the waitress for the check. "That will be great." She searched his face, waiting for him to look back at her. "I really appreciate you getting the estimate and helping me get the job started so soon."

"It's no problem. That's what good neighbors do."

After Lucas paid the tab, he climbed into the front passenger's seat of the little red car, leaving Vivian to chauffeur him home. She talked a little about meeting Mrs. Albertson and Truman, but Lucas simply nodded when she tried to get him to answer her questions. After a few minutes, she finally quit talking. They drove the rest of the way home in silence. Lucas walked her to the door and said goodnight before walking across the street to his own house.

The evening had not turned out as he had planned. He pulled his key chain from his pocket, and his fingers shifted through the keys, easily identifying the one to open the front door. He had planned on swooping in like a knight in shining armor and rescuing Vivian from her house problem. That obviously had not happened. She didn't need him to get what she wanted. What had he expected? Did he think that once he used his time and his resources to remodel her house that she would be eternally grateful and throw herself into his arms?

He walked into his dark living room and flopped down on the couch. Who was he kidding? A woman like Vivian Bradford would never need a guy like him to swoop in and fix anything. He reached over to the coffee table and picked up the picture frame that had been sitting there for the last five years. He didn't have to turn on the light to see the picture. The image was burned into his brain. He was in a tuxedo with a goofy smile on his face, staring down at the woman beside him, dressed in white. He had tried to swoop in and save the day for her too, and look where it had gotten him.

Lucas set the picture down on the table and looked through his front window as a faint light shone through the curtains in Vivian's bedroom window across the street. No, tonight had been a mistake. This entire week had been a mistake. People like Vivian Bradford belonged with people like Finley Parson. They lived in the same world. Not his world.

After a few minutes, the light across the street disappeared and Lucas leaned his head back on the sofa, closing his eyes against the darkness. His world was fine. He had gotten distracted, forgetting how much pain there had been when he had ventured out of his comfort zone. He stood and walked through the darkness down the hall to his bedroom. There were worse things than coming home to a dark, empty house. He felt for the edge of his bed and lay back, pressing his cheek against the cool pillow. There were, but tonight he was having a hard time remembering what those things were.

CHAPTER SEVEN

*V*ivian closed the hymnal and sat back down on the hard, wooden pew beside Mrs. Albertson. She was trying to concentrate on singing the old hymns. They always put her mind in the mood for worship, but her thoughts kept wandering back to her dinner with Lucas on Thursday evening. He seemed to shut down when she mentioned Finley Parson. Before that, they had been having a great time.

When Finley stopped by Thursday morning to introduce himself, she had been so embarrassed for a colleague to see her in her cutoff blue jeans shorts and a tank top, even if she was in her home and he had not been invited. Finley did not seem to mind though, and when he asked her what kind of renovations she wanted to do, she explained about wanting to fix up the home so that one day she would be able to have parties and guests there that would help her grow her law practice.

Finley heard her comment about the shoestring budget too, and suggested she change, and they run to the bank to talk to his father. The meeting had gone well. It had been so nice to walk into a bank and discuss money needs without receiving the condescending looks that Vivian remembered her mother getting from the workers at the Welfare or Food Stamp offices when she was young. She believed in her heart that her mother had done the best for them that she could, and was learning to deal with the animosity she felt toward her parent. Her mother did not seem to know how to handle being thrown into a situation where every whim was not catered to. Still, it didn't take the sting out of the memories.

Mr. Parson listened to Vivian's plans, looked at the amount she had in the bank from Maw Cil, her projected income from her new job, and the amount she needed to borrow. Vivian felt that if Finley Parson had not been there with her, the meeting would not have gone so smoothly. She may would have been able to secure the loan. It seemed that being the granddaughter of Cecille Bradford really meant something in this little town. Even so, a loan officer would have probably required a little more assurance of her financial security that Finley Parson's father didn't ask for. Once he saw she would be working in the same firm as his son, he seemed willing to work with her as well.

Vivian's mind pulled from the thoughts of the loan and back to worship as the young preacher stepped to the pulpit. Mrs. Albertson opened her worn leather Bible up to the passage the sermon was coming from and laid it where Vivian could read along with her. The Good Samaritan. As the preacher began to tell the story, Vivian's mind wandered back to Lucas, and how he had reacted to her news about getting the loan. Shouldn't he be happy that she had found a solution to her problem? Why had he shut down like that when she told him she could get what she wanted?

Vivian shifted her hips on the wooden bench as she looked at the preacher, trying to make her mind focus. Why did she care what Lucas Wade thought anyway? The man still lived with his parents, and he drove a truck as old as he was. After meeting with Langston, Lucas's older brother on Friday, Vivian was pretty sure she had the situation figured out. Langston Wade was the industrious brother who had a successful business. He had probably made up some kind of position for Lucas to have so his little brother could pay his own bills.

No, she needed to keep Lucas Wade at arm's length. He was attractive with his big brown eyes, blonde hair, and easy smile, but that was not enough to let him have any influence over her life. She had goals, goals that Lucas Wade could not help her achieve, nor would he understand them. She would be a good neighbor, but that was it. Thank goodness she started work tomorrow. She would not have to see him again, except to wave hello from across the road.

Vivian started as she felt Mrs. Albertson moving beside her, pulling on the pew in front of them to help her stand on her eighty year old legs. Was church already over? Vivian stood beside her elderly neighbor and bowed her head, embarrassed that she had spent the entire service daydreaming. *Lord, forgive me for not really being here even while I was here. I will do better.*

"Get that pitcher of tea out of the fridge, Vivian." Mrs. Albertson tied her apron around her waist and stepped past Vivian to where her crockpot set on her kitchen counter. She lifted the lid and the tantalizing smell of pot roast with onions, potatoes, and carrots floated into the room. "Let me get the glasses down, and you can put ice in them for us. As soon as this rice cooker goes off, we will be about ready to eat."

Vivian watched as the woman shuffled around her kitchen, leaving her walker near the dining room doorway. "Three glasses?" She took the dark green tea glasses with the short fat stems from Mrs. Albertson's hands. "Are you expecting someone else?"

"Lucas always eats Sunday dinner with me," Mrs. Albertson said, her back turned to Vivian as she shoved a pan of buttered rolls into the oven to brown. "He should be here any second. I saw him talking to that fireman friend of his when we were driving off, but he'll be along shortly."

Vivian bit her lower lip as her eyes darted around the room, unsure of what to do. The last meal she had eaten with Lucas Wade had not ended as well as it should have. She was not looking forward to staring across the table into his chocolate brown eyes for the next hour, but it was too late to back out now. She tucked a wayward strand of hair back into place and straightened the front of her dress. A friendly lunch with a neighbor, that's all this was. He was a neighbor just like Mrs. Albertson was a neighbor. She thought about how he filled out his white tee-shirt and his boyish grin and bit her lip again, suppressing a nervous smile. Well, not exactly like Mrs. Albertson.

Vivian had noticed Lucas talking to a black-haired man and little boy standing with a red-headed woman earlier as they made their way out of the church house to her car. Mrs. Albertson caught her staring at the couple and told her that Blaze Carson had gone to school with Lucas. Wade Construction had built a house for Blaze and his new wife. Several people had told Vivian they were so glad she was moving into Maw Cil's house and how happy that would make her grandmother. Vivian looked at Mrs. Albertson happily puttering around her kitchen. Vivian would be polite and keep the conversation focused on Carson's Bayou and the people in the town. She would get through lunch, then make sure this was the last Sunday dinner she shared with Lucas Wade.

Vivian put the ice in the glasses, poured the tea, and took them into the dining room. When she returned to the kitchen, Lucas was coming in the back door, a white cardboard box in his hand.

"I stopped by the bakery and got a carrot cake for dessert." Lucas set the white box on the counter and stepped over to the kitchen sink to wash his hands. "Miss Lenore said to tell your daughter that she will take as many fresh eggs as her hens will lay."

"I'll make sure I tell her when she calls after while. We always have a phone chat every Sunday afternoon." Mrs. Albertson dipped the gravy from the roast into a terrine but paused to receive a kiss on the cheek from Lucas. "Take this gravy and the rice to the table." She looked back at Vivian. "Honey, if you will get this platter, I will take out the rolls, and we can eat. I believe the preacher talked a little longer than usual today. My stomach is starting to growl."

Vivian's lips turned up into a polite smile as Lucas looked over, noticing for the first time Vivian standing in the doorway. "Hello, Lucas." She picked up the platter, her hands trembling slightly as she brushed past the man, noting a slight scent of citrus as her face turned toward his. She cut her eyes back to the roast and vegetables piled on the platter, determined to ignore the flutter in her chest. "Mrs. Albertson, I haven't had food like this since I was a child. It smells heavenly."

"This is our usual Sunday fare." Mrs. Albertson fell in line behind Lucas and Vivian as they went to the dining room table. Once they were seated, she took Vivian's hand on one side and Lucas's on the other. "Let's say grace before my belly button touches my backbone."

Vivian looked over at Lucas. His hand lay on the table with his palm up, his head already bowed. She slipped her hand into his, and the heat of his touch immediately traveled up her arm. She quickly lowered her head, sure her face and neck were turning pink.

"Lord, we thank you for feeding us with your Word this morning and with this meal this afternoon." Mrs. Albertson's voice filled Vivian's ears as she tried to distract herself from the sensation of Lucas's touch. "We thank you for new beginnings and friendships... and opening our eyes and our hearts so that we can heal in your good time. Amen."

Vivian slipped her hands back into her lap and raised her head. What did Mrs. Albertson mean about healing? Was she talking about everything that had happened with her father? She certainly appreciated the prayers, but she had gotten over the fiasco that was supposed to be her childhood a long time ago. She looked over as Lucas handed her the bowl of rice. "I didn't see your brother at the church. I looked for your mother too. I believe I would recognize her from when I was a kid, but I couldn't find her anywhere. Do they go to a different church?"

"My parents retired to Florida about five years ago." Lucas picked up the terrine of gravy and drizzled a generous helping over his rice. "I thought you knew I owned their house."

"No." Vivian passed the rice to Mrs. Albertson and looked at Lucas, who was staring at the gravy running over his rice. "I guess I assumed you were living with your parents. Now that you mention it, though, I guess they would have cars parked in your garage, wouldn't they?"

"Yes, they are retired, but still very active." Lucas passed the gravy to Vivian, not looking her way. "I was renting a place when they decided to move. It's not my idea of a dream home, but I do like the neighborhood." He flashed a smile at Mrs. Albertson. "Plus, we were in the process of building Langston's house at the time, and he didn't want the place. I knew if I didn't buy it, a stranger would end up living in our family home."

Vivian took the terrine from Lucas's hand, careful to avoid his touch. "I'm glad you bought it. It's nice having someone from my childhood live next door. I lived all over the place growing up. I can't imagine what it would be like as a kid to have a place you knew would always be there." She poured the gravy onto her rice and dipped her pointer finger into the puddle of brown liquid on her plate. She raised it to her lips and looked at Lucas, who was now staring at her with a peculiar look on his face. "I hope and pray that this is my final move though."

"How do you like the gravy?" Mrs. Albertson asked, pouring a generous amount onto her rice, vegetables, and meat. "Roast gravy is my favorite."

"It's absolutely delicious." Vivian lowered her finger and ran her tongue over her lips. She tore her eyes away from Lucas and turned to Mrs. Albertson. "I don't eat a lot of gravy, but I can't imagine any being better than this."

"Langston goes over to the big First Baptist." Mrs. Albertson started energetically mashing her potatoes with her fork. "That's where all the other Wades attend."

"Didn't we pass it on the way to your church?" Vivian took the serving fork from the platter of roast and put a slice of meat on her plate. "That is a very nice building."

"We did. It's the biggest church in town. I enjoy going to see their Christmas production every year." Mrs. Albertson looked from Vivian to Lucas, who seemed to be completely preoccupied with his lunch. "Lucas used to always sing a solo for them until he started coming with Marley to our church."

"You sing?" Vivian looked at Lucas, waiting for him to lift his head.

"I used to," he finally answered, looking up at Vivian. "I haven't in quite a while."

"You haven't in three years." Mrs. Albertson's voice sounded full of compassion as she looked across the table. "I think it's about time you found something new to sing about. Don't you?"

CHAPTER EIGHT

*L*ucas's brow pulled down as he glanced at Mrs. Albertson. "How many times did you move as a child?" he asked Vivian, turning his eyes back toward her, refusing to tackle the subject Mrs. Albertson was trying to open. He had taken the security of his childhood home for granted, never realizing how it would affect him to wonder about where he might be living next year or next month or even next week.

"Oh goodness, more than I can remember." Vivian picked up the green tea glass and took a sip, obviously not wanting to discuss this subject. "I am so excited that your brother has agreed to start on my house tomorrow. You have no idea what it means to me to be able to live in a home that my grandmother has given to me."

"Tomorrow?" Lucas nodded slowly. "I told Langston to make you a priority. I'm glad everything is coming together for you." He listened quietly as Mrs. Albertson told Vivian about different projects she had been involved in over the years with Maw Cil through their church and community clubs. He commented as needed, but mostly watched Vivian out of the corner of his eye.

"Lucas got your grandmother and me involved in the homeless shelter over on Ponte Avenue about ten years ago, didn't you, son?"

"Has it been that long?" Lucas ran his fingers across his chin, remembering when he had first entered the old building to fix the hole in their kitchen ceiling. "I guess it has. That was back when I was a one-man operation, before Langston was out of college."

"You've come a long way since then." Mrs. Albertson's face beamed with pride. "The thing that makes me the most proud of you is that you have never gotten too big for your britches. You own that high dollar construction company, but you still go volunteer at the shelter, and do the repairs for the old folks in our church, and any other folks that need a hand, for that matter."

"That high-dollar company," Lucas said, grinning at the old woman, "allows me to do the kind of work I really enjoy doing every once in a while. Don't make me sound too saintly. I still have plenty of flaws."

"We all do, son." Mrs. Albertson reached over and patted his hand. "But a good man is hard to find nowadays."

"Well, I believe I will step into the kitchen and get the carrot cake." Lucas had a bright red blush on his cheeks as he left the dining room. Mrs. Albertson was obviously enjoying playing matchmaker. He loved the old woman dearly, but she was barking up the wrong tree. Vivian was not interested in him, and... well...

Lucas cut the cake and served the two women before sitting down with his slice. He would make it through that afternoon, but planned to stay away from Sunday lunches until Mrs. Albertson saw that Vivian would never want to date anyone like him.

Two weeks later, Lucas eased the claw of his hammer into place and started prying the tired old molding away from the wall in one of the bedrooms near the back of Maw Cil's house. The smell of ancient damp wood wafted up toward his nostrils as the board creaked away from the wall. A crew started work at the old house on the following Monday, after he had eaten dinner with Vivian and Mrs. Albertson. He had tried to stay away, keeping busy overseeing different building projects around town, but when he came home every evening, as the work crew was leaving Vivian's house, the curiosity of how things were progressing across the street nearly ate a hole in his gut.

He finally gave in and started splitting his workday. He drove to one of the building sites early every morning, staying a few hours, then went to Vivian's house for the rest of the day. In the two weeks since the remodeling started, Finley Parson had been by her house four times. Four times. Why did that man need to drop by like that? If the guy ever lifted a hammer in his life, Lucas would lay an egg and call it George. Didn't he spend all day at the office with Vivian? Wasn't that enough?

Lucas pulled the molding away from the wall and toted it to the pile in the backyard. He would try to salvage as much of the original molding as possible to refinish and put back in the house. Doing this took longer, but it helped keep the integrity of the old home intact, which was important to most of the owners of these old family homes.

"You look a little on the warm side."

Lucas looked over his shoulder at the back-porch doorway. Vivian, dressed in a black form-fitting skirt, white sweater, and black blazer, leaned against the old door frame, her hair pulled away from her face in a sleek chignon. The high heeled black pumps showed off her tanned calves just as the rest of the outfit showed off all of her curves. "You look like a female Perry Mason, except, well..." Lucas ran the back of his arm across his sweaty brow. "Except for all the reasons you don't."

"Good reasons, I hope." Vivian flashed a knowing smile in his direction.

"Yes, very good reasons." Lucas laid the board back down on the pile of molding and stood up, stretching his back. "Everything is coming along well on the house, don't you think?"

"I guess so." Vivian pushed off the door frame, standing up straight. "I know absolutely nothing about carpentry work. It honestly looks like you are all doing more damage than repairing."

"That's all part of the process. We have to tear out the bad to replace it with the good." He stuck the tip of his ring finger between his teeth and tugged off his leather work glove. "We have to put insulation in all these walls, which means we have to do a lot of gutting. Don't worry though. It is probably going to look even better than you are expecting when we are done."

Vivian stepped over to the edge of the porch and looked out across the yard. She reached up and pulled a couple of pins from the back of her head and shook out her mane of thick black hair. "My head gets so tired of having those pins stuck in it all day." She turned her eyes back to where Lucas stood, his eyes watching her every movement. "What? I know this heat makes my hair stringy, but I have got to take those pins out."

Lucas swallowed the boulder that had suddenly formed in

his throat as he watched her toss her head, the afternoon sun silhouetting her hair as it fell to her shoulders. "I... uh... wouldn't." He tried to tear his eyes away as her hair fell around her face, but couldn't seem to get control of his vision. "I mean, it's fine the way it is."

"You can say that because you don't have bobby pins sticking in your scalp for nine hours straight. Finley says it looks more professional up, though, so I guess I will keep wearing it that way."

Vivian reached down and slipped off her shoes. Lucas finally pulled his eyes away, refusing to let his thoughts wander in the direction they were taking him. He had not held a woman in his arms in three years. Those last several months with Marley did not really count in that way, anyway, so it had been closer to three and a half. He watched as Truman's lean yellow form slipped under a dug-out spot under the picket fence near the edge of the backyard, pulling his attention in an easier direction. How old was that cat? At least ten years old.

"Lucas?"

"Huh?" Lucas turned his gaze back to where Vivian was looking at him. "What did you say?"

"I said, I think I want to go with the group that is going to be working on the house for that woman and her little girl that Mrs. Albertson was talking about Sunday after church." Vivian tucked a strand of black hair behind her ear. "She said you were over the team from our church that was helping with the project."

"I am." Lucas stuffed his gloves in the back of his blue jeans pocket. "We are finishing up with the inside this week-end. They should be moving in by next week."

"Oh." Vivian poked out her lower lip. "Am I too late? Mr. Daniel said I needed to get involved in town projects. I was hoping I could help with this one. Our secretary gave me a list of organizations like the Rotary Club, and Lady's auxiliary, Kiwanis Club, and a couple more, but I thought it would be good to do some hands-on work too, especially with the church."

"No." The corners of Lucas's lips tilted up in a slow smile. "There is still plenty to do. You can't wear your high-heeled shoes though. We are definitely a hands-on group."

"Good." Vivian's face perked up. "That is exactly what I am looking for. I don't mind going to the club meetings and things like that, but after being in that office all day, every day, I would rather do something a little more physical on my day off." She stepped back to the doorway. "I'm going to change and then go for a run. Between all the potatoes and gravy I'm eating with Mrs. Albertson every weekend, and the boudin balls I'm having for lunch through the week, if I don't keep running, I will be having to buy new work clothes."

Lucas leaned down and picked up the hammer at his feet as he watched Vivian disappear through the back door. Truman let out a long meow from the steps where he had suddenly reappeared, also watching Vivian's retreating back. Lucas walked over and sat down beside the cat. "Hey, old man. What do you think of this new woman in our lives?" The cat leaned into Lucas's hand as he scratched him between the ears. "Yeah, I imagine neither one of us has any business over here on her side of the street."

"Want a water?" Vivian's voice called from inside the house.

"That sounds good." Lucas stood up as Vivian stepped back onto the porch a few minutes later in a pair of running shorts and a tank top. He let his eyes wander down her frame and then back up before he realized what he was doing. "Where are you going to run?"

"I thought I would make a two-block square." She handed him the water and unscrewed the cap on her own bottle.

"That will keep me in our neighborhood, and I can make as many laps as I want. I looked at the houses when I was driving home. It seems pretty quiet, and I didn't notice a lot of traffic. Want to come?"

"Yeah, might as well, if you will give me a minute to change." He took the water and stepped past Vivian toward the house. "If you decide you don't like running on the road, there's a great park over near the hospital with a jogging route."

"Really? Why don't we give that a try instead? I didn't know we had a park. Finley said he will take me for a drive around town and show me where everything is one Sunday afternoon, but I haven't taken him up on it yet."

"Let me get changed and we will ride over. You need to see the park on foot, not in a car." Lucas peeled his sweaty tee-shirt over his head as he hurried across the road to put on some shorts and running shoes along with a clean shirt.

Finley Parson again. That man wasn't wasting any time on trying to nose into her life, that was for sure.

CHAPTER NINE

One thing was certain. Lucas Wade was easy on the eye. Vivian watched as his shirtless torso disappeared inside his front door. "I don't have any interest in him," she said, looking down at the orange tabby that had followed her through the house and onto her front porch. "We are friends, and neighbors, and well, I'm not hurting anything by looking." The cat rubbed his thin body against her calf and weaved his way between her legs. "Come on. Let me get you some food before we head over to the park. You look thinner than usual."

Vivian stepped inside and pulled the bag of cat food from the pantry. The workers hadn't started on the kitchen yet, or her bedroom and bathroom, but the rest of the house looked like a wrecking ball had come through it. There were rolls of pink insulation sitting in the hallway. The walls around the outer edge of the cavernous living room were knocked out, showing the exterior walls with their dark boards and occasional cobwebs. Some parts already had the pink insulation rolled in place all the way up to the twelve-foot ceilings. They were insulating the walls, windows, and attic. The interior walls would be replaced next before stripping the tired old varnish from the floors, and replacing any boards that were starting to rot. They would check the wiring, put in updated light fixtures, replumb the kitchen and bathrooms, adding showers. The house would be reroofed and painted inside and out. There were other things too, but right now, all she wanted was to get the walls and floors back together. She didn't want to feel like she was living in a warehouse or an old barn any longer than she had to.

"You ready?"

Vivian turned from putting the cat food bag back in the pantry to find Lucas standing behind her in a faded red *Wade Construction Little League Champs* tee-shirt, gray shorts, and tennis shoes. "Let me set his bowl of food on the back porch and grab my car keys."

"We can go in my truck," Lucas said, holding up his keys. "We will be all hot and sweaty after our run. No need to dirty up your nice car."

"Okay." Vivian's voice sounded doubtful. "If we break down on the side of the road, I'm not going for help."

"Florene hasn't let me down yet, and the gas tank is full." Lucas grinned and waited until Vivian returned from putting the cat out. He followed her out the front door and watched while she locked up. "She will get us there and back, don't worry."

"You named your truck Florene?" Vivian pulled on the handle and the passenger's door let out a moan as it opened. "Florene sounds like she's in pain."

"I don't guess that door gets used a lot anymore."

Vivian looked around the interior of the truck as she waited for Lucas to climb in the other side. She laughed as she noticed a cassette player in with the radio and a box of cassettes on the seat between them. "George Jones, Johnny Cash, Willie Nelson? How old are you, fifty?"

"How did you guess? It's my potbelly and that bald spot, isn't it? I am thinking about ordering one of those Bossley toupees off the TV so I can look younger."

Vivian rolled her eyes, looking at his muscular frame and head full of blond hair as he turned the ignition key. *On The Road Again* blared from the truck speakers. He winked at her as he backed out of the driveway. "No, it's because you play your old-man-music loud enough to raise the dead."

An hour later, Vivian climbed back into the cab of the truck, much more tired than she ought to be. They had made one lap around the park, jogging along the edge of the pond where the ducks and swans were paddling around. They continued under the sprawling water oaks, lending shade off and on. They jogged past the side of the park near the back of the hospital campus, then on around to the grassy fields. Families out playing with their children or dogs in the late evening sun made the park seem welcoming.

"I'm definitely out of shape." She picked up the tail of her tank top and mopped her forehead. "A few months ago, I could have run twice as long."

"Well, a few months ago I was in exactly the same shape I'm in today, so I am glad we are done." Lucas popped the Willie Nelson cassette from the player and inserted Johnny Cash. Johnny's deep voice sang, *"I fell into a burning ring of fire,"* and filled the cab as he turned the air conditioner on full blast.

"You have a song for every occasion?" Vivian looked at the box of cassettes between them and picked up one with the words *Marley's music* written in marker across the front.

Mrs. Albertson had mentioned that name a couple of weeks ago when they were eating Sunday lunch together. "Who is Marley?" she asked, holding up the cassette as Johnny and June burned, burned, burned from the dash speakers.

"She is my," Lucas paused, looking at the cassette before turning his eyes back to the road. "She was my wife."

"Oh." Vivian waited for Lucas to continue as the current song ended and Johnny started singing, "*I Walk The Line.*"

Lucas reached over and turned the radio off. "She liked Dolly and Keith Whitley and Tim McGraw, the newer stuff." He stared out the windshield, his knuckles wrapped like a vice around the steering wheel, his jaw now clenched firm in the silence.

"Not a purist like yourself?" Vivian laid the cassette back in the box. Lucas didn't want to talk about this woman, and she didn't want to push him, even though she was curious.

Her mother had such a terrible time when she finally divorced her father. Even though he had been in jail for two years and had eight more years to go before her mother decided to leave him, she had gone through a period of depression that Vivian would never forget. Vivian remembered watching her mother sitting on the love seat like a statue, tears running down her cheeks while the television played whatever Vivian happened to have on.

"Marley used to say I was an old man in a smoking hot young man's body." Lucas chuckled under his breath, finally speaking. "She always knew how to make me laugh."

"What happened?" Vivian bit her lower lip, unsure if she should ask, but curious to find out why the woman had left him? Was it financial troubles? Did she fool around on him? Vivian couldn't imagine Lucas being unfaithful to his wife. She hadn't been around him but for a few weeks, but the boy scout motto seemed to ooze from his pores. Maybe his wife had simply wanted more than he had to give.

"It started out as headaches. She thought she had developed sinus problems, you know?" He glanced over as he pulled up to a stop sign near their neighborhood. "Everybody in this neck of the woods has a little trouble with their sinuses." He pulled in a deep breath. "Then she thought it was migraines."

"It wasn't?" Vivian swallowed hard, her voice suddenly soft with concern.

"She started forgetting stuff and bumping into things. One day she got pulled over for weaving into the opposite lane of traffic, and she admitted she was having double vision." He eased his foot off of the brake and the old truck inched forward toward their houses. "She knew something was wrong, but she wouldn't go to the doctor. Then, one morning in the shower... she had a seizure. I called an ambulance, and..." Lucas's voice faded and a tear ran down his cheek.

Vivian tilted her head forward to see his face. "What happened?"

"The doctors said it was GBM, Glioblastoma. She had surgery and did some chemo, but she died eight months later." He pulled the truck into his driveway and killed the engine. "They said that it was more common in old men." He reached up and wiped his cheek with his palm. "The kind of men that like Johnny Cash and Willie Nelson. Her mother died of endometrial cancer. They think Marley had a gene that made her have a higher risk of getting GBM."

Lucas continued to talk, like a fountain of water gushing from a spout that had been capped for a long time, allowing the pressure to build. "Seems like she would have wanted to go to the doctor earlier after living through her mother having cancer. Wouldn't you think?" He turned and looked at Vivian, searching her face. "Seems like she would have tried to get help, but she kept putting it off. I tried. The Lord knows I tried to get her to make an appointment. She would have a headache and go to bed vomiting and still wouldn't go to the doctor."

"Oh, Lucas." Vivian reached over and touched his arm, unsure of what she should say.

"I should have made her go. I should have made an appointment and loaded her up and taken her anyway." He pulled in a ragged breath of air and stared out the front windshield. "But I didn't."

"It's not your fault."

"I know. The Lord knows when our time on this earth is over." He blinked his eyes, forcing back any more tears. "But if I had taken her to the doctor anyway, maybe it wouldn't have been so bad." He reached his hand up and raked it through his hair. "I'm sorry about all this. You don't want to hear it, I'm sure."

"No, Lucas." Vivian leaned over and placed her hand on his shoulder as he reached for the latch to open the truck door. "Listen, I know we are just starting to know each other again, but we kind of click, like good friends." She paused as he looked back, searching her face. "I know I can be kind of bossy and opinionated, but I can also be a very good listener."

"I appreciate that." Lucas smiled weakly as he opened the old truck door and eased out, slamming it behind him.

Vivian watched as he walked toward his house, his shoulders slumped forward. Poor guy. How long ago had his wife died? Was she from around here? She opened the passenger's side door and slid out as the front door to Lucas's house closed, leaving her alone to walk across the street to her house. She didn't know the answers to her questions, but she knew which neighbor she could talk to and find out.

Vivian walked around the tailgate of Lucas's truck and looked across the road. Finley Parson's Black BMW set parked beside her car. Her brow furrowed as she saw Finley sitting on her front porch swing. It wasn't that she didn't want to see him, not really. She just wanted to sort her thoughts out about what Lucas had told her. She glanced back over her shoulder but didn't see any lights on through the window of Lucas's house. Good. Maybe he had gone to his kitchen to get something to drink, or to his bedroom. Did it bother her that Lucas would see her talking to Finley?

What was Finley? Finley was trying to be a good work friend, and he had helped her get the loan for her renovations. She was grateful for his help and liked him alright as a business associate. No, she was worried about Lucas because of what he had told her. That was all. Like she said, they were good friends... they clicked.

CHAPTER TEN

*L*ucas pulled his old truck to the edge of the yard where the work crews from different churches were gathering. This Saturday should be the last big workday on the house being donated to the homeless woman and her young daughter who were staying at the local shelter. He put his truck in park and killed the engine, letting his eyes roam through the early morning crowds. They liked to get started by six a.m. and work as long as they could. Some, like him, stayed a full twelve hours, while others stayed four or maybe six. Whatever time and services anyone was willing to donate was always appreciated.

He stepped over to where the large group of thirty or more men and women gathered in the front yard for prayer before the workday began. He smiled, surprised as Vivian stepped up from the other side of the yard, but his smile faded as Finley Parson trailed along behind her. Well, there was a first time for everything, and all help was needed, even Finley's. The crowd joined hands as the preacher from the big Presbyterian church on the opposite corner of the Baptist church where Lucas had grown up, led them in prayer.

After the prayer, Lucas grabbed a gallon of interior paint, a roller and a tray, and headed to the dining room. If they could get the walls painted, the toilet installed, and the last few ceiling fans hung, he would come back during the week and do a few final touch-ups so the woman could move in by the following weekend. The churches would come one final time to help her move in and give her housewarming gifts.

Lucas absolutely loved being a part of this ministry and felt that God had drawn him to it to use the abilities He had blessed him with. Last year the churches, along with several civic organizations and company backers, like Wade Brothers Construction, helped to build three houses for local people who either didn't have one, or their homes were falling down around their ears. This was house number two for their current year, and the board of trustees were already taking candidates to start house number three at the end of the summer. He popped the lid off the white paint called Chantilly Lace and poured a generous amount into the tray.

"Need some help?" Vivian stepped up beside him, roller in hand, with a bright smile on her face. Her hair was tied back with a red bandana, and she wore an old tee-shirt that said "Hard Rock Cafe" with a pair of faded, holey jeans. "I refused to learn how to install a toilet, and they wouldn't let me around the electrical projects."

"So that leaves me," Lucas said, smiling up from where he was bent over the paint tray.

"That leaves you." She watched as he gently pushed the roller across the tray, coating the thick nap with a generous coat of the Chantilly Lace paint. "Is there any special technique for getting the paint on the wall that I should know about?"

"You want to get enough on your roller to put a nice even coat on the wall, but not so much that it drips and runs." He lifted the roller to the wall and painted a W, then continued rolling, filling in the space.

"Nice even coat, no drips and runs. Got it." Vivian dipped her roller into the tray and attempted to mimic Lucas's motion for loading the roller. She lifted her roller and poked her lips out like a duck, as the paint dripped from the roller and ran down her arm. "What did I do wrong?"

"Here." Lucas set his roller on the edge of the pan and stepped behind her, reaching around to help her properly hold the paint roller. "See, not so much pressure." He breathed in the beachy smell of her hair as he leaned in behind her, guiding her hand as she pushed the paint roller through the pan. "Then you roll the excess out here at the edge of the pan." He felt the warmth of her back against his chest as he lifted her hand, holding the paint roller from the pan. "See, no dripping." His breath fell near her earlobe, and a few strands of loose hair that had slipped from the bandana tickled his lips. He tried to swallow, but his mouth was suddenly like a desert.

"No dripping," Vivian repeated, her voice husky.

"Now, you step over here." Lucas continued to stand behind her, one arm draped around her shoulder, his hand over hers as they held the roller. His other hand rested on her upper back. They stepped closer to the wall as his hand moved from her back down to the small of her waist. "Now you just nudge the roller against the wall." He paused, guiding her arm. "Not too much pressure, gently, let the roller caress the wall so the paint will stick without dripping."

"Caress the wall." Vivian whispered, goosebumps appearing on her arms as Lucas breathed the words into her ear.

"Anybody want donuts and coffee?" Finley Parson stepped through the dining room door with a giant cardboard tray of glazed donuts. He stared at the couple in the corner of the room.

Lucas jumped back from behind Vivian, stepping into the paint tray behind him. His work boot splashed into the white paint as Vivian slung her arm around, slapping her roller against the side of his face.

"It's a good thing we put the drop cloths down," Lucas said, wiping the white paint from his eyebrow and side of his face. "I don't think you quite have the hang of it yet." He looked at Vivian, who was biting her lower lip, her eyes stretched wide as she looked at the paint dripping from his eyebrow to his chin. He wasn't sure if she was going to laugh or cry. "We usually try to only get the paint on the wall."

"You look like you are ready to enter the circus," she finally said, her face breaking into a smile. "I am so, so sorry, Lucas, but at least I didn't drip it down my elbow this time."

"Why don't you grab a coffee and a donut, Lucas." Finley said, stepping over to the paint can as he took a bite of the freshly glazed donut. "I'll finish teaching Vivian how to paint."

"Do you know how to paint?" Lucas blew a puff of air from between his lips as paint tried to drip into his mouth.

"Uh, yeah," Finley said, a slight smirk on his face. "I believe I can handle it."

Lucas grabbed a rag from a stepladder near the wall and wiped his face, then reached down and wiped his boot. He was careful to stay on the drop cloth until there was no danger of getting paint on the floors. He glanced over his shoulder at Finley as he lifted the roller from the pan. The paint dripped from Finley's roller onto the drop cloth as he reached for the wall and haphazardly slapped the paint against the surface. Oh well, he would fix the man's mess later. He needed to get a little space between him and Vivian, and changing shoes was a good excuse to make it happen.

After Lucas rinsed the paint from his face at the water hose in the front yard, he took off his work boots and pulled on his rubber boots that were in the back of his truck. They weren't very comfortable, but he didn't want to waste time going home to change. He went back into the house, but headed to the bathroom to help with the plumbing. Let Finley and Vivian do the painting. He could put a second coat on the wall later after they were done if needed.

An hour later, Lucas handed the monkey wrench to one of the other men and headed up the short hall to the dining area. He watched as Vivian lifted the overflowing roller pan and attempted to pour some of the paint back in the bucket. "Need some help?"

"Oh, man." Vivian looked up and smiled, the end of her nose white with paint, along with several strands of hair. "If you don't mind. The paint poured a little faster than I thought it would."

"Where is your teacher?" Lucas stepped over and took the roller pan from her hands and poured the majority of the paint back into the bucket. "Did he teach you everything you need to know and leave you to it?"

"Not exactly." Vivian grabbed her paint roller and rolled it through the pan, coating the roller with much more precision than she had the last time he watched her. "He got a phone call right after you stepped out and had to leave." She stood up and made a W on the final section of the dining room wall. "But I think I've about figured it out. Mrs. Batson showed me how to do the trim too." Vivian smiled and nodded her head in the direction of the wall she had just completed. "I think it looks pretty good."

Lucas looked around the room, noticing that she had gotten the crown molding painted, as well as the molding at the bottom. "You've been a busy woman." He turned back and picked up a paintbrush in a plastic cup sitting near the roller pan. "I can help, and we will get this room knocked out before everyone breaks for lunch." He picked up the step stool and brought it over to the wall where she was rolling. "You should have come and gotten me. I didn't know you were working in here by yourself. I could have come back and helped. There are plenty of men in there getting the bathroom done."

"I didn't mind. It was kind of nice to be able to paint and simply listen to the snatches of conversation around me."

"Hear anything interesting?" Lucas stepped onto the ladder and began carefully painting the crown molding with the Chantilly Lace white. The ceiling was also a shade of white, but it was a high gloss. Most people wouldn't notice the subtle difference in the colors if he happened to spill over onto the ceiling, but he would. He painted this little two-bedroom house with as much care as he had the mayor's mansion back when he worked on it.

"A couple of the ladies told me that you are the one that got this house building ministry started a few years ago." Vivian reached her hand up and wiped a stray strand of hair from her cheek, smearing white paint onto her face from her fingertips. "They said it kind of blossomed from some hurricane relief efforts."

"Yeah. When Xander came through and ripped up this area, our shelter was full for a long time. After we helped people who had flood and wind damage, I got to thinking, and decided that there are other people around who are in need of a hand up even when a natural disaster hasn't taken their homes." Lucas glanced around at the little dining room with the connecting kitchen area. "This little house will get Devina Adams and her daughter out of the shelter and let her raise her child in a home. She was living with her grandfather, but his dementia got so bad he had to go into the nursing home. When he went, so did his check, and she couldn't afford the rent working at the dollar store."

"Does this group just give her the home? How do you decide who you build a house for?" Vivian looked up where Lucas was painting the trim again. "Is there some kind of criteria a person has to meet to get one of these? My mother and I sure could have used one when Daddy... left."

"The person has to be drug free, holding down a steady job with a good work history, and not have a criminal lifestyle." Lucas dipped his brush back into his plastic cup for more paint. "If the person has some kind of record, we don't automatically dismiss them off the list. They do have to show that they are no longer involved in a criminal lifestyle. Some people fall on hard times and make bad choices. We also encourage them to attend church, but we don't force ourselves on them. Devina is working at the dollar store in the evenings and going to the community college during the day to get a vocational nursing diploma."

"Lucas Wade, you are a pretty special guy." Vivian looked up to where he leaned across the ladder to paint the molding above the window. "When you get through with my house, it's going to be extravagant and beautiful, but you put the same amount of care into these little homes as well, don't you, even though you don't make a single penny off of them."

"Everybody needs a home. A place where they know they can go to and feel safe. From what you've said about moving around, you should understand that."

"Oh, I understand it." Vivian's brow creased as she thought about her enormous house and compared it to the place they were working on. "I'm ashamed to say that I've never taken that understanding and used it to help make other's situations better like you have."

Lucas looked out the window where the group was gathering around the ice chests and getting their sandwiches and chips out for lunch. "There are some things in this world that I can't make better," he said, his voice taking on a hint of sadness as he continued to stare out the window. "When I work on changing the things I can for the better, it takes my mind off the things that I can't change."

CHAPTER ELEVEN

*V*ivian pasted on a polite smile as she headed past the secretary of her law office and hurried into the parking lot in the dim evening twilight. She knew the woman was waiting for her to finish her work so she could lock up behind her, but she couldn't help it. Mr. Denver, the senior lawyer who hired her for the position, was really piling the work on. She was determined to stay caught up and make a good impression on her new boss.

She glanced down at her phone as she unlocked her car. Six-thirty. No wonder the woman was aggravated with her. Everyone else in the building left at least two hours ago. Vivian would order flowers to be delivered to the secretary tomorrow to make up for having her stay late. Hopefully she could talk to Mr. Denver about getting her own keys to the place. Each lawyer owned keys to their office and their files, but it seemed that this particular secretary was the only one with a key to the entire building.

She rolled her head around on her shoulders as she slid behind the steering wheel of her red sports car. She had been in Carson's Bayou three months now, and things seemed to be going along as planned. Well, not exactly as planned. She backed out of her parking spot and her eyes crinkled in a sad smile as she thought about last night.

Her house was just about finished, and her life would be changing. Most evenings, no matter how late she worked, she would find Lucas still somewhere in her home finishing up a bit of carpentry, plumbing, wiring, or whatever was needing to be done. They would usually talk for a few minutes, and after she changed clothes go to the park for a run. She had not realized how much she had grown used to this routine until last night, when Lucas announced that everything should be completed when she got home today. Maybe that's why she had stayed so late. Maybe she was avoiding going home to her big ole empty house.

Vivian pulled into her driveway and glanced across the road to Lucas's house as she got out of her car. His dirty old truck was parked in its usual place. She didn't see any lights on in his house, but that didn't really mean anything. He could be in the back somewhere, and she wouldn't be able to tell if he was home or not. She left her briefcase on the passenger's seat and grabbed her purse. She still needed to get some work done, but she was not in the mood. What was she in the mood for? Not running, at least not by herself.

"I didn't think you were ever going to get home."

Vivian's eyes shot up from looking at the keys in her hand, searching for the one to the front door. She stared through the twilight to the other end of the porch where Lucas's voice was coming from. Her eyes searched through the ever dimming sunset as a firefly darted across the yard. There he was, lounging on the swing, head on one armrest, legs stretched across to the other one, gently swaying like he had nothing better to do than wait for her to get home.

"Comfy?" she asked, pulling the house key from her

keychain. She started to stick it in the hole, but turned the handle instead, realizing the door was probably unlocked.

Lucas swung his legs to the porch floor and stood from the swing in one fluid motion. "Actually, not too comfortable. You need to get a pillow for the swing. That wooden arm is kind of rough on my neck."

"I will have to do that before you come over for your next nap." Vivian pushed open the door and walked into the foyer, the aroma of something warm and tantalizing wafting through to her nostrils. She glanced over her shoulder as Lucas flipped on the light switch behind her. "What have you been up to?" Her eyebrows shot up as she really looked at him, taking in the expensive looking black suit, white shirt, and silver tie. "My, my, you clean up nicely, Mr. Wade. I've never seen you dressed up before. I didn't know you owned a suit."

"I only bring it out for special occasions." Lucas shut the front door and took Vivian's purse from her arm, placing it on the hall table. "Why don't you go change out of your work clothes while I put the French bread in the oven."

"What smells so wonderful? I didn't know you knew how to cook." She stared down the hallway toward the kitchen door, noticing how clean and shiny the walls and floors were. This morning, even though the area was already completed, there was still a thick coat of sawdust on every surface, and scraps of wood had been laying on the floor against the wall with other things that needed to be cleaned up. "Someone has been very busy."

"You go change," Lucas said, stepping between her and the hallway, blocking her line of vision. "I will take you on the tour after we eat."

"What should I wear?" Vivian looked at Lucas again. "You look like you are going to a wedding or a photo shoot for GQ, I'm not sure which one."

"Slip on some shorts and a tee-shirt. Get comfortable and come to the dining room."

"The formal dining room? Not the kitchen?"

"Yes, the dining room." Lucas placed his hands on her shoulders and steered her through her bedroom door off to the right. "I'll see you in a few minutes."

Vivian watched as he shut the door in her face, then turned to look across the room to her closet. "Tee-shirt and shorts, my eye," she whispered, kicking off her black pumps and unbuttoning her white shirt. She stripped down to her slip as she hurried across the room to her closet, leaving a trail of shoes and clothes as she walked. There was no way she was going to sit across the table from Lucas dressed in a tee-shirt and shorts with him looking like that.

She flipped through her work attire and pulled out something she had not tried on since she had made the purchase, her little red dress she had splurged and bought after graduating from law school. She bought the dress, hoping to wear it one day. She thought she would wear it to celebrate her new job as a lawyer in a prestigious firm in Atlanta, where she was living at the time. Well, that hadn't worked out like she had expected, but she was a lawyer, and she was celebrating. At least it felt like she was. She slipped the dress from the hanger, laid it on the bed, and stepped into the adjoining bathroom to freshen up.

Fifteen minutes later, Vivian's white heels clacked across her newly refinished hardwood floors which ran down her hall, through her kitchen, and into the formal dining room. She had not bought furniture for this room yet, so why were they going to the dining room? A broad smile stretched across her face as she looked at the little square table covered with a lace tablecloth, adorned with white taper candles in crystal holders. Lucas's broad shoulders bent over the three candles as he lit them. The table was beautifully adorned with crystal stemware she had never laid eyes on before. As he stepped to the side, she noticed a serving dolly with china plates and bowls that were also unfamiliar to her. "How did you do all of this?" she asked, stepping over to the table. "This is lovely."

"Don't you worry about that." Lucas pulled out a chair and waited for her to sit, then placed a plate of steaming lasagna in front of her. He set a second plate on the table for him, then sat down in his chair. "I was supposed to make a salad, but I forgot, so we have lasagna and bread and dessert. Hope that will do."

"Salad is overrated." Vivian's eyes sparkled as she looked through the candlelight. "I can't believe you went to all of this trouble for me."

"I know how much it means to you to be moving into your own home." The corner of his mouth turned up in a lopsided smile, causing a dimple to appear in his cheek. "I wanted your first night in your finished house to be special."

Vivian thought back to a couple of months ago, when she had gone with him to the little house they helped build for the young woman and her daughter. The volunteers cleaned up the house and helped the woman move in the few pieces of furniture they had gathered up from garage sales and secondhand stores. They also brought pizza and ate with her, celebrating her new life in her new home. "Has anyone ever told you that you are a special guy?"

"Not lately." Lucas poured iced tea into their glasses. "I wanted to be a part of this night with you. When you remember the first night in your new place, I want you to look back on it with a smile, and I want to be a part of that memory."

"I just put on fresh mascara," Vivian said, touching her fingertip to the corner of her eye. "Don't make me get all weepy." She sucked in a deep breath of air and looked across at Lucas, his brown eyes reflecting the soft candlelight. "When my dad got arrested for embezzling that money... when they put him in prison, my life changed. After he wasn't in the picture anymore, I never had a real home. We were always moving, and sometimes." Vivian pulled her eyes away from his and looked down at her hands resting on the lacy tablecloth. "Sometimes we slept in our car, or in a shelter like the one you talk about here in town." She looked up again, this time not bothering to try to stop the tears threatening to spill from her eyes. "When I graduated from high school, my mother told me I had to go to work and do something to help pay the bills. I worked as a waitress and attended college on student loans. After the first semester, I moved into the school dorms, but my mom still expected me to help with the bills. When she was unable to pay the rent *again*, though, and was forced to move, I didn't move with her. I stayed at the dorm, kept working and going to school, determined that I would do whatever it took to make my life stable... normal."

"Did your mother have some kind of habit she was supporting?" Lucas asked, his voice filled with compassion. "Is that why you were always moving and never had enough money?"

"No, not like you think. She just couldn't get it together. When Daddy was with us, she lived a spoiled and pampered life, eating out almost every meal, buying stuff she didn't need, things like that. When he was taken away, and the money left, she tried to continue living that lifestyle. She would go out to eat steak at a ridiculously expensive restaurant one night, and not have money to pay the light bill the next day." Vivian shrugged her shoulders. "When I told her I wasn't moving again, she left me, and three months later she remarried."

A tear spilled from her lashes and trailed down her cheek,

splashing on the table. Lucas leaned in, his eyes searching hers as his hand brushed away the tear. "I'm so sorry."

"It's okay," she whispered, looking down at his lips, so close to hers. She tilted her head ever so slightly, closing her eyes, allowing her lips to brush against his, soft and warm, as he moved his head closer.

Lucas's hand stayed on her cheek, his lips on her lips for only a second before he pulled his head away and sat back up. "I'm sorry. I didn't mean for that to happen," he said, blinking several times and rubbing his hand across his jaw. His eyes pulled away from her face and he looked down at the plate in front of him. "We better eat this lasagna before it gets cold."

As Lucas pulled away, Vivian stared across the corner of the table, trying to wrap her mind around what just happened. Her tongue eased out and ran across her bottom lip, drinking in the taste his kiss had left there. Her mind swirled with the scent of spice and citrus cologne that lingered from where he had been so near only seconds before.

"You want some bread?" Lucas picked up the basket with slices of buttered French bread and stuck it awkwardly in her direction.

"Uh, yes. Thank you." She took a slice of the crusty bread from the basket and tore it into, focusing her eyes on the food, the tea glass, anything but the kiss that had her heart doing a backflip. Why was she sitting here in her red cocktail dress in the candlelight, having dinner with Lucas Wade? Lucas Wade was not in her plan... but that kiss....

CHAPTER TWELVE

*H*e was playing with fire. He knew that, but no matter how often he told himself to stay away, he found himself seeking out Vivian Bradford. There was no reason for him to have set up the dinner for her last night. He could have supervised the cleanup, put the spare key under the rock where she kept it, and headed back across the street to his own house like a man with good sense.

Once the idea popped into his head to make the night special, like the mission team did for the people they built the homes for; however, he just couldn't let it go. He had wanted it to be really special, too. What was up with that? No pizza and cans of Coke. No, he had spent all morning getting his and Marley's wedding china and crystal down from the attic. Every once in a while, he ran across the street to make sure the clean-up was going as it should. He also had to make the meal. He only knew how to cook three things: pancakes, brownies, and lasagna. He wanted to make it himself, so lasagna, salad, brownies and ice cream for dessert were the obvious choices. Of course, he forgot the salad. He almost ran to McDonalds to get a couple of prepackaged ones and dump them in a bowl, but time had been running short, or so he had thought.

The workmen finished the cleanup and were gone by five. He had hustled everything across the street, set it up, changed into his suit, and walked to Vivian's front porch to wait for her by six o'clock, the time she had been pulling into her driveway for the past two weeks. By the time she drove up at six-forty, he was having serious doubts about what he had done, and even more doubts about why he was doing it.

There was no doubt; however, that he was seeking her out every chance he got. He could tell himself he had been managing the work crew, and that he needed to stay late at her house to make sure everything got done. He could try to convince himself that he had been planning to start exercising and her offer to be his jogging partner happened to fit into that plan. He could tell himself that the moon was made of cheese, or that Chuck Norris wasn't the coolest Texas Ranger on the planet. He could try to convince himself of a lot of things, but he knew he was not being honest with himself.

If there was any doubt that he was falling for Vivian before last night, the kiss had taken it all away. He didn't even have to close his eyes to imagine the way her lips tasted on his or the way the feel of her cheek in the palm of his hand caused his heart to pound. The scent of her skin as he closed his eyes last night, wanting to draw closer to her and lose himself in that moment... it was all still right there with him this morning.

He ran his hand through the top of his hair trying to push the memory of the kiss to the back of his mind where it belonged. He pulled into a parking spot on the old side of town between the coffee shop that opened up last spring, and the gift and flower shop that specialized in handmade lotions and bath accessories. The town council was really pushing to improve this side of town. Mrs. Albertson had mentioned that somebody bought the old bank building next door to the shelter and was going to turn it into a nice restaurant. Carson's Bayou seemed to be coming back to life on this side of the railroad tracks, and that was a good thing.

Lucas climbed out of his truck and went into the coffee shop to get a couple of coffees to go before heading across the street to the shelter. One of the caretakers had asked him Sunday if he would drop by this week to check on one of the bathrooms because the floor seemed to stay damp around the toilet. The caretaker also served as the handyman, but thought he needed a second opinion before he ripped the commode out of the floor. Lucas had been so busy, actually preoccupied with Vivian's renovations, and had not gotten around to it yet. Today, though, he didn't have a reason to put the man off. He didn't mind going to the shelter anyway. He had come to know a lot of the regulars there, and it was time to visit them again.

"I believe I want an iced coffee today, Sarah, for a change."

A smile formed on Lucas's lips as he stepped inside the coffee shop, hearing the voice that drew him like a kid to a candy store. He stepped up a few inches in line behind Vivian, listening as she placed her order. She wore her usual black skirt for work, but today she wore a pink ribbed sweater and did not have on the blazer. Her hair was twisted up in that tight knot. The one she said made her head hurt. The one Finley Parson liked. If he pulled that chopstick from the center, he felt sure her hair would tumble down on her shoulders. His hand raised from his side with this thought, but he caught himself and lowered it.

"Hey, Lucas, your brother left about ten minutes ago." Lucas jerked his eyes from the back of Vivian's head to the young woman who was looking past Vivian and talking to him. Vivian turned at the sound of his name and her cheeks turned a becoming shade of pink as he smiled at them both.

Was she thinking about last night, their kiss?

"Lucas?" Sarah said his name again, a look of laughter on her face. "Did you hear me?"

Lucas felt the heat slipping up his own neck this time. "Hey, Sarah. I'm sorry, my mind was on something else. What was Langston doing? I haven't been into the office yet this morning."

"He was getting coffee. He comes in several times a week." Sarah looked back at Vivian. "Yours will be up in a second, Viv. Do you mind if I go ahead and take Lucas's order?"

"Oh," Vivian looked up from where she had suddenly gotten preoccupied with something in her purse. "Sure, go ahead. I will just sit over here."

Vivian smiled shyly at Lucas and stepped away from the counter. Lucas placed his order for two large black coffees. He paid for the drinks with cash and told Sarah to keep the change before he stepped to the side to allow the two women who entered the coffee shop behind him to place their orders. Yes, putting this coffee shop here had been a stroke of genius for somebody if the place stayed this busy all the time.

Lucas walked over to the little glass top table by the window near the front of the shop. "Mind if I wait with you?" He smiled down at Vivian, who sat scrolling through her cell phone.

"No, of course not." Vivian set her phone beside her and waited as Lucas took his seat. "Your office is around here?"

"It's a few blocks over, in the old Stanford building. We bought and renovated it several years ago. I lease part of it to a CPA since we don't need all that space."

"That's not far from my office," Vivian said, a look of surprise crossing her features. "When I called your brother to get the estimate for the house, we did everything over the phone. He brought me the papers to sign at my house since he said he needed to look at it, anyway. I didn't realize you had such a nice workplace."

"It's an excellent piece of property," Lucas said, nodding his head. "I've restored a lot of these older buildings, and their owners have turned them into thriving businesses. I think it's important our town keeps as much of its history intact as possible. One way to do that is to renovate these older buildings whenever we can, instead of tearing them down and putting up a cookie-cutter new one."

"You sound kind of passionate about this," Vivian said, raising her brow as she smiled. "Seems there's a whole lot more to you than the guy I first met covered in dirt and mud."

"Maybe." Lucas grinned. "I'm really just a man that loves his hometown, I guess." He paused as Sarah called Vivian's name. "Well, maybe I'll see you later. We can still plan on running this evening if you want to."

"That would be nice." Vivian pushed her chair back from the little round table and stood. "Lucas, I wanted to thank you for dinner last night. You made me feel so special, and, well." She bit her lower lip and looked down at Lucas. "I haven't felt special in a long time."

"You're welcome." Lucas's voice was tender, touched by her words. "If I made you feel special, then I accomplished something, but Vivian." He reached over and touched the back of her nearby hand with the tip of his finger. "You should always feel special."

Sarah called Vivian's name again, and she turned and walked to the counter, not speaking again. She paid for her coffee and turned to go, nodding her head in his direction before walking out the glass door.

Yes, he was playing with fire. He could feel the heat in his finger where he had touched her hand, but more than that, he could feel a deep burning in his chest. A burning that was even stronger than the flame that was there when he was married to Marley. That flame had sputtered and eventually drowned into a memory of sadness and loss. He thought he would never feel anything in that place ever again. Now he was thinking, no, hoping that he was wrong. Vivian was putting down roots here. She had no plans to move away, so there was no risk of her leaving and taking his heart with her.

He looked through the front glass as she walked down the sidewalk out of sight. He had not planned on ever giving his heart away again. As a matter of fact, he had built up a few walls to make sure it didn't happen. It hurt too much when someone else held your heart. Even if they didn't do it on purpose, they held the power to break it into a million pieces, like Marley had done the day she lay in his arms drawing her last breath.

He thought of all the long, lonely nights since then when he lay staring at the ceiling somewhere above his bed in the darkness, of all the meals alone, with the ticking of the kitchen clock to keep him company. The little flame now burning in his chest made him want more than what he had.

"Lucas?"

Lucas turned, surprised to see Sarah standing beside him with his coffees.

"I called your name a couple of times, but you didn't answer." She set the cups in front of him. "Everything okay?"

"Yes." He pushed back his chair and stood, looking down at the petite blue-eyed blond. "Everything is getting better all the time."

CHAPTER THIRTEEN

Things were going so well. Yes, she was working her fingers to the bone, but wasn't that the plan? Mr. Denver, the senior partner, had already told her she had more drive than anyone hired there in a long time. Since Finley Parson was the last lawyer brought into the firm, and that had been two years ago, she was pretty sure the statement was directed against him.

If there was something that was not going great, it was her relationship with Finley. The problem was, Finley seemed completely incapable of understanding that she was not interested in dating him. Three weeks ago, she happened to mention to Mr. Denver that her house renovations were completed, and now there should be a little more time in her schedule for social activities. She had been thinking about hosting parties and dinners in her home to help raise her status in Carson's Bayou, and bring in more clients. Finley, who was standing nearby, apparently assumed she meant there would be more free time for dating in general. The most annoying part about the whole thing was he didn't hint around that he wanted to see her. He didn't even ask her out.

He simply assumed she would jump and run when he told her he had made plans.

"I'll pick you up at seven on Friday, and we'll drive to that seafood place near the coast," Finley announced, coming into her office that morning.

"I can't, Finley." Vivian tried to keep her voice cordial, hiding the irritation grating on her nerves every time he made his presumptuous date plans. "I am already busy."

"You know, I've asked you out four times over the past three weeks, and we haven't gone out yet."

No, you haven't asked me out once, you clod. You assumed I would go and announced your plans to me.

Finley flopped his lanky frame into the leather chair across from her desk. "Check your calendar and see when you are free. I wouldn't do this for anyone else, but set the date, and I'll clear my schedule for you."

"Finley." Vivian tilted her chin down, trying to keep her features pleasant. He did help her out with her loan, and he wasn't a bad guy, really, just annoying. "I need to get back to work. I'll try to look at my schedule and see when we can go to lunch—maybe next week."

"Lunch? And then come back to work?" Finley rolled his eyes and sat back up in the chair. "Vivian, I understand that you are trying to impress old man Denver, but if you keep working like you are, you will be old before your time, and that would be a shame."

"Lunch. Next week, Finley. Okay?" Vivian watched as he stood from the chair. "But right now, I really must get back to work."

"I guess that will do, Viv." He looked down as he stepped away from her desk and winked. "But I am not going to let you forget about it."

"No," Vivian whispered, watching Finley turn and stroll out of her office. "I don't imagine you will." She stared down at her computer screen, then at the tray full of papers to her left. Where to start? Mr. Denver's secretary came in that morning and laid a file on her tray, telling her she needed to familiarize herself with the lease of some building. She hadn't said it was urgent, so Vivian had tossed it on the growing pile and continued on the current project that she needed to finish.

She reached into the tray and took out the folder. Good Samaritan House. That was the name of the shelter across the street from the coffee shop. The building was actually an enormous, old three-story brick home someone had renovated in the past. They had turned it into a place for the down and out of Carson's Bayou to take refuge.

A frown creased her brow as she read through the papers. The three-year property lease would be up for renewal in two weeks. The board that ran the shelter had renewed the lease twice before, occupying the building for the past six years. According to what she was reading, they were very good tenants.

Vivian bit her lower lip as her eyes read through the document. The owners of the property were not offering to lease the building again. The proper paperwork was delivered to the Good Samaritan House board a couple of weeks ago, telling the renters they would have to be cleared out of the place in thirty days.

She slowly laid the papers back on the tray as she thought about everything Lucas had told her about Good Samaritan House. Several local churches, charitable organizations, and businesses around town supported the place. He had not actually said so, but Vivian had a feeling that Wade Brothers Construction was one of the shelter's biggest contributors. One Sunday afternoon, when Vivian and Mrs. Albertson were having lunch, her neighbor bragged that Lucas did more to help the needy in their town than any other single man around. Even though Lucas had not come back to eat with them again since the first time she was over, the old lady continued to sing his praises and play the matchmaker every chance she got.

Did Lucas know the Good Samaritan House was being evicted? They went jogging every afternoon when she got off work. Their conversations often centered around Carson's Bayou. One thing she had learned about Lucas from these chats was that he had a passion for helping others needing a leg up during hard times. Surely, in all of their talks, if he would have known about the shelter having to move, he would have mentioned it.

She picked the papers up again and flipped to the page where she had stopped reading. Her eyes darted back and forth across the page as she realized why Mr. Denver sent her the lease information and other paperwork. The board of the Good Samaritan House was meeting that evening, and he wanted her to attend as a representative of the property owners. Mr. Denver was going to make her be the hatchet man; make sure the board understood they were required to evacuate the premises in two weeks.

Vivian swallowed, trying to push down the rock hard lump forming in her throat. It was possible that the people she was meeting with already knew they had to move. After all, the document said that the owners delivered the proper notice in the proper time frame. The building owner's legal representation at the board meeting might merely be a gesture of good will to make sure the transition happened smoothly. The lump in her throat refused to move, causing a tightness in her gut. No, this whole thing gave off a vibe of bad news. She was the newest person in the firm, the one with the least amount of connections in the town. Who better in the firm to deliver news that would make all the churches and other good-hearted people in the town madder than wet hens?

Vivian pushed her chair back and stood up from the desk. She grabbed the papers and stepped out of her office, walking in swift strides to Mr. Denver's office down the hall. She would go to the meeting. It was her job, and she needed her job, but she was not going in there uninformed. There was a reason why the owner of the firm was sending the newest member to attend such a public meeting. There was a reason... and she was going to find out what it was before five o'clock when she had to be there.

$\mathcal{V}$ ivian looked down the table toward Lucas, his anger visible to everyone there. She pushed down the urge to turn and run out of the room, run away from Carson's Bayou, from him, from this whole situation. How had things gotten so complicated in such a short amount of time? She pulled in a deep breath, trying to breathe in a courage that she did not feel.

"All they had to do was pick up the phone and give me a call." Lucas threw the papers on the scarred up old wooden table and leaned back in the metal folding chair, irritation evident in his every movement. The other board members of the Good Samaritan House turned their eyes from him to the other end of the table, where Vivian waited. The crowded room looked more like a storage closet than a boardroom, and the tension was so thick it could be cut with a knife.

"If you look at the postmark, you'll see that they sent the notice out within the legal time frame that the agreement specifies to notify you of termination of the lease." Vivian lifted her arm and stretched it in the direction where Lucas sat holding the paper, making sure her business voice was firmly in place. "I can ask the owners to give you another couple of weeks to get everyone moved."

"I'm not saying we didn't get the letter in time." Lucas stared down the length of the table into Vivian's face, his voice deep with agitation. "Mrs. Frances said she got the letter. She just assumed it was the lease renewal and brought it tonight for us to vote on. We had no reason to believe that we would not be signing for another three years."

"It's on the first page."

"Vivian," Lucas said, interrupting her well planned out response. "Listen to me. This may be legal, but it's not right. We always pay our rent. We have made tremendous improvements on the property at no cost to the owners. We are good tenants." He raised his hand and drug it across his clenched jawline. "They have no reason to make us move except for one—and I would like to think that I am wrong for even considering that reason. These people have no other place to go."

"The same group that is renovating the building next to this one and making it a restaurant has offered to buy this building," Vivian said, careful again to keep the emotions churning inside her chest hidden from everyone in the room. "The owners have decided the property will better serve the needs of the changing community in the hands of these buyers."

"Miss Bradford." Mrs. Frances, the gray-haired woman who had smiled so warmly at Vivian and welcomed her into their meeting only twenty minutes ago, now looked at her completely deflated. "They think the homeless shelter will somehow drive away customers from their restaurant, but they're wrong. The people who will be eating at that restaurant are the same people who help raise the money to keep this shelter going. We spend our money in Carson's Bayou, and we support the people of Carson's Bayou... in times of excess, and times of need. Can't you see that?" The woman's mouth turned up into a sad smile. "We need to help the people in the shelter, not push them away."

"I'm sorry." Vivian's eyes moved from one board member to the next. They stopped on Lucas, who was staring at her, regret settling on his face like an unwelcomed visitor. "There's nothing I can do," she said, regret sneaking into her voice. "The shelter is going to have to go."

"Thank you, Miss Bradford, for coming tonight, and making sure we understood that the lease is not going to be renewed." Brother Jacobs, pastor of the Presbyterian church, and current chairman of the board for the Good Samaritan House, nodded at Vivian. "If you don't mind, we will let you find your way out. We need to discuss how we are going to handle this move."

Vivian looked at the pastor and pushed her chair back from the old table. The metal chair made a scraping noise on the wooden floor of the storeroom. Everyone in the room was dressed casually, like they were meeting with friends, not attending a business function. Everyone but her. These people were part of the backbone of Carson's Bayou that worked together to try to make their town a better place for everyone in it. She was the outsider.

"I hope you can find a place to relocate the shelter," Vivian said, looking around the room with a weak smile. "I'm sorry I had to meet some of you this way." She looked at Lucas. He stared at her. His face no longer showing hurt or anger. Her brow wrinkled as she tried to understand the look on his face. Indifference? Regret? "I really am sorry."

CHAPTER FOURTEEN

"*I* still can't believe she did it." Lucas sat on Mrs. Albertson's front porch the following day drinking a glass of sweet tea. "She had on that black skirt and jacket with her hair pulled back in that tight knot like she was in some kind of battle uniform. Then she attacked without a hint of mercy."

"Have you tried to talk to her about it?" Mrs. Albertson picked up her sweaty tea glass from the little wicker table sitting between the two old rocking chairs. "Maybe there's some way you can save the shelter if you two will work together."

"No." Lucas drained the last bit of tea from the green glass and set it on the table. "I was so upset after that meeting, I figured I'd better stay away from her. Besides, I don't know where she went. I didn't see her car pull into her house until around eleven last night." He picked the glass back up and swirled the melting ice cubes around. "Do you think she doesn't understand what will happen to all the people living at the shelter if we can't find them another place to stay?"

"I'm not sure, son." Mrs. Albertson looked toward the

ancient oak trees shading her front yard as well as the quiet street. A squirrel darted down the trunk of the tree and sat in the grass, shaking its tail, no fear at all for the occupants of the porch. "But I do know that you need to let go of your anger and seek the Lord in all of this. I feel certain that Vivian is not doing this out of meanness. She probably feels that she doesn't have a choice. She did just start that job, remember?"

"But she's better than that." Lucas jerked his hand holding the tea glass forward, tossing the few pieces of ice out into the grass. The squirrel froze for half a second, then darted back up the tree, out of sight into the branches. "I know she thinks she has to drive that fancy little car, and dress like she stepped out of a television show, but deep inside, I have to believe that she knows those things are not who she is." He set the glass down again and looked over at Mrs. Albertson. "She has to know that those people at the shelter are so much more than *the homeless people*. I've seen the real her, and it was not that woman in the board meeting last night."

"Lucas, honey, you have to remember that Vivian had a very different growing up than you did."

"I know but..."

"Now listen a minute." Mrs. Albertson reached over and squeezed Lucas's forearm. "She's all alone in this town, and she's running as fast as she can from a past that she feels she has been wearing on her chest like a scarlet letter. I'm not making excuses for what she did. All I am doing is telling you that you need to look for the way the Lord would want you to handle this."

"Are you saying we should turn the people in the shelter out in the streets without a fight because Vivian Bradford is insecure about who she is?" Lucas's eyes searched Mrs. Albertson's face as he reached up and rubbed the back of his neck. "You know I can't do that."

"No, boy." Mrs. Albertson pushed her lips into a frown. She watched as Lucas fell back in the rocker and starred up at the ceiling. Her voice became soft. "I simply want you to show her the same compassion and Christian love that you show those homeless folks. She has a roof over her head, but I don't think she feels she has a home any more than them folks do. If we turn on her right here at the first sign of trouble, will we be acting any better than she did?"

"What should I do?" Lucas sat forward and looked across the yard, not really seeing what was in front of him.

"First of all, you should pray."

"I have. I asked the Lord to let her see that what she is doing is wrong."

"That's good," Mrs. Albertson said slowly, "but have you prayed for yourself? Have you asked God what you can do to make this better? Have you yielded yourself to him so he can use you in this to help bring Vivian closer to God?"

"No." The words were barely more than a whisper as Lucas absorbed what his neighbor was saying. "All I've thought... and prayed about, is how I can stop this from happening."

"Lucas, I know you care about that girl. I saw it on your face the first time you talked about her. If you care about her, you need to pray for the Lord to bring her into the proper relationship with him. Pray that he will use you to help her as he sees fit. Don't make yourself her enemy. Let God make you into an instrument that He can use to do his will in this situation."

"I guess I need to talk to God some more before I try to talk to Vivian." Lucas pulled in a deep breath and blew it out slowly. "I don't know what I'm going to do if we can't figure out a way for the shelter to stay in that building."

"God knows, Lucas. That's what you have to remember. You don't know, but God does."

Lucas sat on his front porch in the dim twilight Sunday evening watching the occasional firefly light up, then disappear. It must have been getting close to nine o'clock. Yesterday, after leaving Mrs. Albertson's, Lucas had loaded up his gear and drove down to Lake Adderly in the neighboring parish. He had spent the rest of the day fishing and praying. He hadn't caught anything, but the point of the trip had not really been to catch fish.

When he had gotten home that evening, Vivian's car was in her yard, but her lights were not on. It was just as well. He wasn't ready to talk to her yet. Every time he thought about how she sounded when she told him and the rest of the board members about the lease being terminated, his jaw clamped down, if not in anger, then at least in agitation. She had sounded like she was explaining how to take out the trash or meet some sort of financial obligation. She had been completely without emotion... and it had torn a hole in his heart.

He had not seen her at church earlier today, but her car was in her yard now. He had been sitting on the porch for close to an hour, willing her to come outside. So far, her place was as dead as a tomb.

He stooped forward in his chair, elbows on his knees. She was probably sitting over there in the dark, feeling terrible about what she had done. She had probably come to her senses by now. If he explained to her that they could work together to straighten all this out, she would say she was sorry, and then he could help her convince the owners of the building to let the Good Samaritan House buy the place outright. He had decided today, after thinking about what he needed to do, that this was the best plan of action. After all, he had the money, and should have tried to buy the place six years ago when they first agreed to put the shelter there. Back then, that side of town was pretty run down, and if he had made an offer, he was sure he could have gotten it for a great price. Now he would have to pay through the nose for it, but he would do it to save the shelter. He felt a small flutter in his stomach as he sat back up. If he walked over and talked to Vivian... helped her get out of this mess, she was sure to be grateful too. They could mend their fences and get things back to how they were.

Lucas held his hand up to his face, sheltering his eyes. Car lights flashed as they turned onto the block and rolled slowly down the street in his direction, blinding his vision. A black BMW pulled into Vivian's front yard. Finley Parson got out of the car and walked around to the passenger's side. He opened the door and took Vivian's hand. Her legs stretched out of the car, and she stood up in her red dress, the dress from *their* dinner. Lucas watched, mouth gaping open, as the couple walked to the front steps, standing as if on a stage in front of the car's headlights. Vivian looked up at Finley and smiled before she released his hand. Finley said something else, and she smiled again.

After what seemed like an eternity, Finley got back in his car and drove away. Lucas strained his eyes, trying to see what Vivian was doing as his vision adjusted back to the sudden darkness. He heard a squeaking sound, and his eyes darted over to the porch swing.

He felt himself standing up and walking across his yard. Somehow, his body was moving in her direction, probably the last place in the world he needed to be going right now feeling the way he felt. She had played him for a fool two times in three days. He had sat on his front porch all evening feeling sorry for her, getting ready to come over like a knight in shining armor and bail her out of the mess she had gotten herself into. The whole time he had been sitting over there, getting ready to spend his hard-earned money so she would not look like a jerk, she had been out wining and dining with Finley Parson.

"Have a nice time?" Lucas stepped onto Vivian's front porch and looked down at where she sat in the darkness. Her silhouette moved and his eyes found her face. "Nice dress."

"Thank you. It's the only one I have for special occasions." Vivian's voice drifted through the darkness, sadness making the words move slowly, like a drip of molasses.

"And this was a special occasion." Lucas stepped closer to the porch swing and watched as Vivian instinctively pushed back away from his advance. The swing went back a few inches, then swung back forward bringing her near again. "When you weren't home Friday night, and I didn't see you at church this morning, I figured you were ashamed to show your face." Lucas heard the words flowing from his lips and knew he should stop, step back, go home and calm down, but the words came out anyway. "I see I was wrong. You were out celebrating your victory with your chosen side."

Vivian's back straightened as her voice took on the seek and destroy tone Lucas instantly recognized. "I was working. You know what that is, don't you? It's something I have to do twenty-four seven, not only when I want to, like you do. It's so easy to sit over there in your little yard and judge me when everybody in this town loves you. You don't have to worry about who you are or where you came from because you are the great Lucas Wade." Her finger reached up and poked him in the chest, driving home her words. "Lucas Wade, savior to the downtrodden."

"You know what? Forget it." Lucas turned and started

back down the steps. He paused as the sound of Vivian's heels hit the wooden porch, hurrying behind him.

"Oh, no, you wanted to tell me something. Well, here I am." Vivian grabbed his upper arm and waited for Lucas to turn around. "I'm not a coward and do not run from a fight. If you have something to say, say it."

Lucas turned and glared down at Vivian's hand. He slowly raised his eyes to her face. "You want to know what you are? Fine. You are a selfish schemer, exactly like your father. You only care about yourself and don't have a clue about what really matters." Lucas paused as Vivian's eyes stretched wide, stricken, like he had slapped her in the face. "Now kindly let go of my arm so I can go home where I belong.

CHAPTER FIFTEEN

*V*ivian leaned forward, giving in to the piercing pain in her side. Her hands rested on her knees and she pulled air in and out of her lungs in a controlled manner. Control. She controlled her breathing. She could, and would, control the rest of her body too. The pounding in her chest started to slow as her breathing brought the oxygen into her body, easing the cramp in her side caused from the long, hard jog.

A drop of sweat dripped off the end of her nose, and she slowly raised her head and looked across the park. The sun was starting to peek out from behind the trees. She straightened back up and lifted the back of her arm to her forehead, mopping the sweat from her brow.

Running had always been her go-to mechanism for dealing with emotional overload. She ran away the embarrassment of watching the mailman stare at her with pity when he delivered her mail postmarked from the penitentiary. She ran away the anger of witnessing her mother spend the water bill money on a designer handbag, then not have any water to take a shower before school until the next payday. She ran away the fear of moving to a new town and starting over, all alone. Why couldn't she run away the ache in her heart that started Friday night when she saw the disappointment in Lucas's eyes?

After leaving the Good Samaritan House Friday, she had driven around for a while trying to decide what to do. She eventually ended up back at her office, using her new key to get into the building. She reviewed everything Mr. Denver had given her on the lease agreement again, finding nothing ethically unsavory in the way their clients were handling the changes. She studied the background of the people who owned the building. She investigated their reputation as landlords, and anything else she could get her hands on about the situation.

Lucas was correct in saying the board for the Good Samaritan House were great tenants. Upgrades to the house and grounds occurred frequently, improving the value of the property. The charity had paid for all the changes, adding up to a tidy sum over the past six years. The owners definitely slanted the lease agreement to work in favor of the landlords, but that was nothing new. Later that night, while lying in her bed, she kept telling herself that this was only a business decision by business savvy clients, and she had done nothing wrong.

Saturday, with puffy eyes and an extra-large cup of coffee, she had driven all the way to Lafayette and bought new furniture for her living room and formal dining room. She knew exactly what style of furnishings she wanted for the place. She had watched a few makeover shows and looked in several magazines over the past few weeks in anticipation of decorating the rooms after the repairs were completed. When she found out about her grandmother giving her the house a few months ago, she had been so excited to be able to set up her very own home. Picking out the furnishings that reflected her taste and style should have been fun, but the trip had not lifted her spirits like she thought it would have.

Then, Sunday afternoon, Mr. Denver called asking her and Finley to join him, his wife, and another couple at the country club for dinner. She had not wanted to accept, but what could she do? He was her boss; this was the type of thing she had been trying to achieve ever since... well, ever since she could remember. To be looked upon with respect, because she had done a good job, to be accepted into a group where she was able to hold her head up and be proud. This was it. When Mr. Denver suggested that she and Finley come together, she felt she had to agree. Finley's parents, the bank president and his wife, happened to be the other couple Mr. Denver had invited.

Vivian walked back across the edge of the park to her waiting car. A few more joggers were starting to show up now. Only the ones who ran for the love of running got up this early. She had been a sunrise runner all through college, but when she moved to Carson's Bayou, things began to change. She still loved to run, and enjoyed running every evening with Lucas, but if she was honest with herself, the need to run off the tension had eased a little since she came to the small town. It had, at least, until this weekend. She unlocked her car and pulled her water bottle from the front seat. She would need to get home and shower soon so she could make it to work on time, but for a few more minutes, she needed to breathe and slow down her pounding heart.

At the dinner, Mr. Denver asked how her meeting with the Good Samaritan House board had gone. He praised her for a job well done when she told him the board's plan to move the shelter without disputing the departure deadline. Her butterfly shrimp tasted like sawdust as she listened to her colleagues talk about how moving the homeless shelter would help drive up the value of the surrounding properties. She could barely stomach her crème brûlée as Mr. Denver and Mr. Parson laughed. They congratulated themselves on hiring such a brilliant, beautiful bulldog of a lawyer. They even made a couple of wisecracks about Finley needing to take lessons from her on how to be a hardnose and get things done.

When, on the way back to her house that evening, Finley mentioned that Mr. Denver and his father were two of the largest investors in the new restaurant opening up next door to the shelter, things finally began to fall into place. A clenching spasm started again in her gut as she thought about the situation she was in.

Was Lucas right? Was she a selfish schemer like her father? She helped work on the house for that homeless woman. That wasn't selfish. *Unless you are doing it with a selfish motive, like to impress the people around you.* Vivian's eyes squeezed shut as she leaned against the edge of her car and gulped down her water.

She did not go to church yesterday. Lucas was right about that. She had been too embarrassed to show her face, sure that Mrs. Frances had shared the story of the board meeting with everyone at the church. She listened on the radio to the preacher from her old church in Atlanta instead, and his words still stung her to the core.

"Are you storing up your treasures in heaven, or here on earth? Are you more concerned about what your coworkers and peers think about you than what your heavenly Father thinks about you?"

The coffee and toast Vivian tried to swallow almost gagged her as the sermon rang out in her kitchen that morning. She had jumped up from the table and changed the channel to a Christian music station, but when an old hymn began playing, she felt like she was being chased by snapping hounds. The singer's voice declared that she would rather have Jesus than anything this world could afford today. Was that her conviction as well? She ended up turning the radio off completely, storming back to her bed, and going back to sleep. She had been exhausted. That had to be why everything seemed to be making her feel so out of sorts.

Now; however, the convictions still lingered. Was God trying to speak to her? Was she running away from Him this morning too? She climbed into her car and picked up her phone, typing in *treasures in heaven* in the search bar. Matthew chapter six popped up on the screen and Vivian started to read, her mind drinking in the teaching of Jesus as thirstily as she had gulped the water a few minutes before.

Tears dripped down her cheeks. There was so much in that chapter that seemed to have been written just for her. She felt like the Matthew chapter six poster child... and the poster was not a pretty one. She was trying to serve two masters. She was storing up treasures on earth instead of heaven, and she was definitely anxious about everything. How did she end up this way? When did it happen? It didn't matter. She knew the only way to fix it was to give the whole ugly, embarrassing mess to God. Her head bowed low, finally yielding her will to her Father, not the one who let her down all those years ago, but to the one who held her up through all of the troubles... when she hadn't even known he was doing it.

Vivian started the car engine and pulled onto the street toward home. What could she do about the shelter? All the paperwork for the eviction was perfectly legal. Mr. Denver had made sure of that. Plus, if she tried to go against the two men, and somehow figured out a way to keep the homeless people in that building by stopping the sale of the property, Mr. Denver would fire her. Mr. Parson would call in her bank loan. They would run her out of Carson's Bayou, and she would be an embarrassment to her grandmother, just like her father had been. Lucas was right. In her efforts to try to be different, to rise above and do better, she had ended up like her father after all.

She pulled into her yard and glanced across the street at the old pickup truck Lucas seemed to love so much. The look in his eyes when she explained the lease agreement on Friday night flashed into her mind. The sound of his voice when he confronted her on Sunday night rang in her ears. Would he ever forgive her? Even if he did, he would never want to have the kind of friendship they had before. Her heart ached at the thought of losing his friendship. It hurt even more as she realized she wanted more than friendship. He called her a selfish schemer, and now she could see that he was right. She hadn't meant it that way, had not even realized she was acting that way, but it was all too late to fix now.

Her tennis shoes walked quietly up the porch steps, where she pulled out her key and unlocked the door. A touch of warm softness brushed against her leg, and she looked down. "Truman, you are up early." She opened the door and the cat walked in ahead of her with slow, languid steps. What was it Mrs. Albertson said? Nobody owned the cat, the cat owned the neighborhood. She watched as Truman headed down the hall and through the kitchen doorway in search of a meal.

The gleam of the new wood shone as she flipped the switch and the chandelier high above sent light cascading down into the room. Her home resembled a showplace now, something any person would brag about. Anyone would feel honored to live here. She pulled in a deep breath. She had done everything in her power to clean up her act, fix her outside, show the world that she deserved to be there. All the while, her insides were what needed fixing.

This house did not represent who she was any more than all the apartments and rental houses she and her mother had been run out of over the years. The clenching in her gut began to loosen. She had so much to do, and no idea how to do it. It was okay though; she was not alone, and even though she didn't have a plan, for once in her life, she was not scared of not being in control.

A long, soulful meow came from the kitchen and a smile formed on Vivian's lips. She had to feed her house guest. That was first. After that, she would step out on faith.

CHAPTER SIXTEEN

One week later, Lucas sat behind his desk, stretching his arms out in both directions, trying to release the tension running across his shoulders. A tap at the door drew his gaze across the room as a man with features very similar to his own stuck his head through the door.

"Bro, we need to talk." Langston Wade stepped into the office and shut the door behind him. Even though the sandy blond hair and chocolate brown eyes looked so similar that it was almost like looking in a mirror, the two men were hardly ever mistaken for each other around town. It wasn't that the brothers did not physically favor one another. They definitely did. Of course, the way they dressed was completely different, but it went deeper than that. It was the way they carried themselves, their presence of being that was so different.

Langston's long legs crossed the room in two strides. His expensive white button-up shirt, red tie, and suit pants looked as natural on him as the tee-shirt and jeans did on Lucas. When Langston entered a room, he immediately drew attention to himself. Not on purpose, it was simply who he was. Lucas finally realized in his early twenties that his brother didn't even realize the effect he had on people. Langston was born to take charge, to lead, to run things, and it showed.

People were drawn to Langston's confidence, to his ability to assess a situation, break it down, and come up with a solution. Langston reminded him of a towering oak tree, casting a protective shadow over every person he came in contact with. Lucas had grown up in that shadow. He didn't resent his brother for being that way, but for a while it had been difficult to figure out who he was... who he really was, without being who Langston thought he should be.

"I'm heading out after lunch to check on that crew over in Calver Parish." Lucas pulled his lips together, suppressing a yawn as it tried to escape. "I'll be gone for the rest of the afternoon. Is there something I need to do before I head out?"

"No." Langston sat down in the chair on the other side of the desk. "Look. You've spent more time in this office over the past week than you have in five years. I know this thing with the shelter has you upset, but hiding away is not the answer." Langston never minced words. Sugar coating any situation was a foreign concept to him.

"I'm not hiding."

Lucas puffed out his chest, feeling the need to drum his fist against it. He looked across the room to the windows of his office that overlooked the street below. The morning sun poured into the room, and from where he sat, all he could see was the bright blue sky with a few white clouds behind the tops of the buildings across the street. If he wanted to see the people below, he actually needed to get out of his chair, walk over, and look down. He had been doing that about once an hour, scanning the street and the sidewalk for a little red car, or long black hair dressed in a black skirt and blazer.

"I'm trying to be more of a presence here at the office." The explanation sounded ridiculous, even to his ears.

"Why don't you go talk to her?" Langston laced his fingers together in front of him as he assessed his brother through narrowed eyes. "I know she's a lawyer, and from what I've heard, she is pretty ruthless."

"She's not ruthless," Lucas cut in, shaking his head. "She is just... determined."

"Okay. Determined." Langston's brow furrowed. "Little brother, you can't let one hardheaded woman undo everything you have thrown your heart and soul into since Marley's death. That's not like you." He paused, leaning against the front of the desk, not the least bit concerned that he was invading his brother's personal space. "Do you want me to go talk to her? I can set up a meeting, see what we can do for your shelter. Have you thought about buying the building yourself?"

"Yes, I thought about it. I've even looked into it." Lucas scrubbed a hand over the whiskers on his jaw. He must have forgotten to shave this morning. "The sale is already pending. The purchase was made hush hush, just like the handling of the ending of our lease. Wallace Denver manipulated the entire situation to get the building away from us. There's nothing I can do. The shelter is going to have to close, at least at that address."

"So, you are throwing in the towel and hiding in your office."

Langston's voice sounded so sure, and so accusing, causing Lucas's eyes to jerk up from where he had been staring over at the window.

"I'm not hiding, Langston. You don't know what you're talking about. I talked to Vivian right after all this happened last Sunday night. I figured I would buy the place, like you said. I waited for her to get home so I could go over and tell her I had figured out a way to solve our problem. I was such a jerk to her after she finally got home from her date with Finley Parson. She didn't want to hear what I had to say."

"I see." Langston eyed his little brother, understanding suddenly flashing in his eyes. "What exactly did she say when you told her your plan?"

"I..." Lucas pinched his lips together and looked past his brother to the door, wishing he would leave and not make them talk about this. "I didn't tell her. I got mad and told her she was acting like her father. You know what happened with Maw Cil's son, don't you? That's her father."

"Yeah, I know." Langston's voice softened as he looked at him. "Okay, I'm going to tell you something, then I'm going to get out of your business."

"Really?" Lucas raised an eyebrow. "That will be a first."

"Yes, but I need you to listen to me without any of your little brother attitude."

"I'm all ears." Lucas leaned forward in his chair, trying not to roll his eyes. "Give me your years of wisdom."

"When Marley died, I watched what happened to you. The way you coped seemed to be going around and rescuing people in hopeless situations."

"I..."

"Listen." Langston held up his hand and continued. "The way I figured it, you couldn't control what happened to Marley. You couldn't rescue her, so you started rescuing everybody else. Brother." Langston paused, his eyes searching Lucas's face. "You can't rescue everybody. Some people don't want to be rescued—and some people have to rescue themselves, or they will keep falling right back into the same pit." He raised his palm and nodded at Lucas's wrinkled tee-shirt, unshaven face, and uncombed hair. "Have you ever thought that maybe all this stuff you are doing for other people is actually for yourself? And now that you've found a woman who doesn't need you to save her... it's making you deal with your own real brokenness?"

A tight knot burned in his gut. "What do I do, Langston? I think I am in love with this woman. It's like a reverse "Where's Waldo." Everywhere I go, I see her. She was even coming out of the shelter yesterday morning. I can't stand to be around her after the things I said to her. She has to hate me but... I can't stand to be away from her, either. And then there's the shelter."

"Are you sure you want to be involved with a woman who would help throw homeless people out on the street? She doesn't sound like a Christian, or the type of woman you would want to spend your life with either."

"She's not like that. I know her, I'm sure of it." Lucas ground his hands together. "She's in over her head... and I don't know how to help her."

"Have you considered that maybe it's not your place to help her?"

A frown fell across Lucas's face. "What do you mean? Of course, I need to help her."

"Let me put it another way, then. What if God doesn't want you to help her in the way you think you should help her? Have you considered that God might be putting her through something, and He doesn't want your nose in it? Maybe He doesn't want you jumping in trying to straighten things out until He has done everything He is trying to do."

"Oh." Lucas raised his eyebrows.

Is that what Mrs. Albertson had been trying to make him understand when she said to pray for himself and ask what God wanted him to do? Did God really want him to step back and give Vivian space?

"What do I do?" Lucas took a long breath, attempting to ease the tension in his gut. "I don't know how to *not* do something."

"First, go home and clean yourself up. You look awful." Langston pushed himself up from the chair. "Then pray. Let God do what needs to be done in this woman's life... with or without you." He slapped his hands together and watched as Lucas started to rise from the chair. "Come back when you're ready, and let's start looking for a new place to put the shelter." A smile spread across Langston's face, making him look more like his little brother than he usually did. "Let's work together to find the new place for the Good Samaritan House. You aren't the only person in Carson's Bayou who can do a good deed. But this time we are going to buy whatever building we decide to use, or we will buy land and build a place. No more renting."

"Yes, sir, boss." Lucas stood up, feeling better than he had in over a week. He watched his big brother stride out of the room, closing the door behind him. Lucas walked to the window, not seeing anything that was happening out there because Langston was right. And that stung his pride because he was doing exactly what he had accused Vivian of doing. He was acting in his own self interest in the name of helping others. There was nothing wrong with all the things he was doing for other people, but the bottom line was, he really wasn't doing it all for other people. He was doing it all for himself, to make himself feel better.

On the day Marley died, the burden of failure had fallen across his back like a cloak, and he had worn it ever since. He had used her death to block out other people who wanted to come along beside him and help him work through his grief. Instead, he dove into the one thing he loved to do, build. He had used that love, and his grief, to help the homeless, but at the same time, the work had kept him from turning his loss over to God. It was time to let the grief go.

He looked down at his wrinkled tee-shirt and blue jeans, stained with paint and grease. No wonder their secretary had given him such a pitiful stare when he came into the office. He fished his keys from his pocket and hurried out to his truck. On his way out, he called the foreman of the crew he was going to inspect to reschedule for another day.

Lucas looked for Vivian's little red car as he drove past her law office, but didn't see it in her usual parking spot. He turned at the stop sign and made a block, driving past the coffee shop. Sure enough, her little car was parked along the street. He started to pull in behind her but thought better of it and eased the truck on down the road.

What would he say to her?

Hey, I think I love you, and by the way, I've decided to mind my own business? How lame of an apology was that?

He searched for her long black hair through the glass storefront of the coffee shop, but he didn't see her. As he pulled past the shelter, Mrs. Frances was coming out the door, and behind her... Vivian. That was two times in a week that she had been to his shelter. Well, it wasn't *his* shelter.

But what was she doing here? He turned his head and shamelessly stared as he drove past. Vivian seemed to be listening intently to something Mrs. Frances was saying. Both ladies looked at ease, much more at ease than they had at the board meeting.

What was going on?

CHAPTER SEVENTEEN

*F*OR SALE. Lucas felt his jaw drop as he pulled into his driveway. He jumped out of the old truck and trotted across the road to Vivian's yard, his mind racing as he read the sign again. It couldn't be. He raked his hand through the top of his hair, and his eyes darted around the empty yard.

She couldn't sell. He remembered her saying that Maw Cil's will stipulated that she could not sell the house. His legs carried him slowly, mechanically back across the street, past his truck with the door still open, into his house.

She must have found a loophole in the will. That had to be it. What else could it be? He climbed into the shower and let the hot water slam into his face like tiny needles, trying to open his mind so he could comprehend Vivian's plan.

After a few seconds, he finally turned away from the water and began to wash his hair as his brain started to function again. If she was selling the house, she must be moving out of Carson's Bayou. Maw Cil's house was her only connection to this town. He slapped the soapy washcloth across his back with a vengeance as he thought about his conversation with Mrs. Albertson. Carson's Bayou was not her home, she didn't really have a home.

The washcloth dropped from his hand and splattered against the shower floor, forgotten as the events of the past few weeks played over in his head. When she moved into the house across the street, he had pursued her, there was no denying this. He had been there every day when she got home from work. He had encouraged her to get to know him better, to become his friend. She had finally opened up a little about her past, not a lot, but she was starting to. When something happened, and their friendship hit a bump in the road... he had used her past against her. He had abandoned her, leaving her to the likes of Finley Parson.

Lucas stepped out of the shower and started drying off. Langston said that maybe she didn't want to be rescued, and more importantly, God's plan might not include him rescuing her. He couldn't stand by and do nothing while she moved away... out of his life. Surely that wasn't God's plan. He stepped into the bedroom and slipped on a pair of jeans and a wrinkle free tee-shirt from his closet.

What had Mrs. Albertson said that night? If he turned on her when she needed him, he was acting exactly like she had, turning on the homeless people when they needed her. His betrayal was worse. She had never professed to care for the people at the Good Samaritan House. She had not portrayed herself as their friend before turning her back on them. He had said he was her friend, acted like he cared for her, but when she didn't behave the way he expected, he abandoned her, shoved her to the outside, acted like an enemy.

Lucas sat on the edge of the bed, his eyes closed. Maybe it was time to do what Mrs. Albertson said. He needed to pray for himself, really pray, not rant and rave about how he was trying to live like he should, complaining often about the problems that kept tripping him up. He kept making excuses for his behavior and then pointing out Vivian's problems so God could hurry up and take care of those. No, he needed to repent, come clean. He slid off the bed and onto his knees, a place he had not been in a long time, too long.

Three days later, Vivian walked through the doors of the Good Samaritan House and breathed in the aroma of gumbo and freshly baked cornbread. Mrs. Frances called that morning, asking her to attend the board meeting that evening. The two women had met several times over the past week, a couple of times at the shelter, and a couple more at the older woman's house. Vivian's plan had been to set everything in motion, then let Mrs. Frances be the spokesperson, telling the board what she was doing. She had no desire to face the group again, particularly Lucas. She had seen his truck in his driveway across the street several times, but he had not made any attempt to come over and talk. She wasn't surprised— not really.

It had taken a few days to get her plan set up, and now her world was turned completely upside down. It didn't matter, though. She honestly felt more free, more at peace than she had in, well, in forever. She walked through the common room of the shelter where a TV sat in the corner. A couple of mismatched couches and chairs of different styles set around the room for the residents of the shelter to sit and visit, or watch TV, or read, whatever they wanted. It was a homey space, with afghans over the backs of the chairs, and magazines on the coffee table.

She heard talking and an occasional laugh as she walked back to the dining room where the twelve current residents of the shelter were either in the food assembly line being served, or on the other side of the table helping serve. Mrs. Frances stood behind a pan of cornbread, her silver hair covered in a little black net, clear plastic gloves on her manicured hands, passing out generous squares of cornbread to the last few people in line.

"Vivian." A warm smile crossed Mrs. Frances's face as she looked to the doorway where Vivian was standing, looking unsure where to go. "Fix yourself a plate and then you can follow me to the boardroom. Everyone is back there eating before we start the meeting."

"I brought these." Vivian stepped up to the serving line and showed Mrs. Frances her Target bag full of white cotton socks. "They were having a sale, and I figured you could give them out as needed."

"That's so generous of you." Mrs. Frances slipped off her plastic gloves and stepped from behind the serving line. She took the bag from Vivian and set it on a nearby table. "Lacy will make sure they get put away when she finishes eating."

Vivian took one of the colorful trays. It reminded her of the many school cafeterias she had been in as a child. She proceeded through the line, dipping a bowl of gumbo, grabbing a piece of cornbread, and adding a scoop of potato salad. She knew the locals all plopped their potato salad in the center of their gumbo, somehow eating the two completely different flavors together. She had not quite gotten up the courage to try that yet. She dropped her scoop into one of the little side sections of her square plate. After setting a sweaty plastic tumbler full of ice-cold sweet tea on the corner of the tray, she proceeded to follow Mrs. Frances from the dining room. They maneuvered their way into the back, where the board members sat in the crowded little storage room around the old wooden table.

Vivian swallowed the small lump in her throat as she

stepped into the room and set her tray down. The soft chatter that had been going on when she entered the room fell silent as she slid into the chair beside Mrs. Frances. The woman insisted that she come to the meeting, telling Vivian she needed to be there to explain the details of the plan and answer any questions.

Vivian looked down at her tray, not meeting the eyes of the board members, or the pastor of Maw Cil's church—her church, who was also there with his wife. She closed her eyes and sent up a prayer, asking for a blessing for her food and wisdom to proceed through the rest of the night.

The talk began to start again as she lifted her head. Glancing around, she could feel one set of eyes drawing her as she looked across the table. Lucas, sitting further down on the opposite side, stared at Vivian. She took in his smooth-shaven jaw, his sandy blond hair, getting a little long and curling up at his collar, and then his eyes, peering at her—drinking her in. The look on his face caused her heart to pound, but the small smile that turned up the corners of his lips sent a shiver through her stomach that she had not felt since the last time they had shared a meal together.

Vivian tried to eat the tempting food on her tray, but the butterflies in her stomach wouldn't allow it. She listened to the chatter around the table as the longtime residents of Carson's Bayou talked about who was sick in the hospital, how friends and relatives were doing in the local nursing home, and other topics of interest about the people they loved in their little town. She waited for Lucas's voice, keeping her eyes trained on the other faces in the room, but he offered little to the conversation, only giving short answers when someone asked a direct question.

She expected to feel hostility toward her because of what had happened the last time she had been in this room, but as the people continued to talk, she realized that it wasn't there.

Mrs. Frances had assured her she would not reveal her plan until tonight, just in case it fell through. Maybe her new friend had asked them all to treat her kindly, in spite of her past actions. She looked at Mrs. Frances sitting beside her, hair net still in place. Hopefully, one day, she would have a heart like Mrs. Frances. One that showed through to others, even when they didn't understand what she was doing.

Finally, the board meeting was called to order. The Presbyterian pastor explained that Mrs. Frances had been meeting with Vivian. Because Mrs. Frances had requested, Vivian was being allowed to address the board again tonight. He nodded in Vivian's direction, encouraging her to speak.

"Thank you all for hearing me tonight." Vivian cleared her throat as she looked around the room at the faces. A few had guarded expressions, waiting to see what bomb she would drop on them this time, but none looked angry. "A lot has changed since the last time I talked to you. I hope these changes will help you to continue your ministry of caring for the homeless in Carson's Bayou." She pulled in a deep breath, fighting the tears that wanted to clog her throat. The urge to step into her role as a detached lawyer, and continue with a speech that would be strictly business, burned inside of her, but she pushed it away. A hand reached under the table and gently squeezed hers. Vivian looked over at Mrs. Frances, who nodded at her with an encouraging smile.

"As I'm sure all of you know, I moved here when my grandmother passed away, and I started living in her house. Over the past few months I have taken the money she left me, plus some more that I borrowed from the bank, and renovated the house so that it is completely modernized and, well, extravagant, with an industrial kitchen, and beautiful molding and light fixtures... really nice."

Vivian looked away from the faces, all staring back at her, turning her eyes to a shelf behind the table where an enormous can of pork and beans set. "I put the house on the market earlier this week. Once the sale goes through, all the money will go to the charity fund at Philadelphia Baptist Church here in town where my grandmother attended." Vivian looked over at Mrs. Frances, who still held her hand. "I have talked with Mrs. Frances about this. She feels certain that the church will use the money to help find the Good Samaritan House a new building if I request they do this with the donation."

Vivian could feel more than hear a collective sigh of relief around the table as she said the last sentence. Questions began coming from all directions as everyone discussed her proposal. Yes, there was an offer already on the table for the house. Yes, it should be sold soon. Yes, the money should be enough to purchase another place for the shelter that would meet their needs. No, she wanted nothing in return. Vivian continued to answer each question as it was presented, but her mind waited, listening for the one voice she needed to hear. Finally, when she couldn't wait any longer, she looked down the table, looked at his face. His eyes stared back into hers, warm, soft, understanding. A silent thank you formed on his lips, and a smile formed on hers.

CHAPTER EIGHTEEN

$\mathcal{A}$fter the board meeting, Lucas walked Vivian to her car and followed her home. He followed her up her steps and sat beside her in the twilight on the porch swing. "What made you decide to sell the house?" He nudged the swing with the toe of his cowboy boot, causing them to sway in the darkness. "It's not your fault all of this happened, you know. Walter Denver and Floyd Parson already had everything set up to get that building away from the shelter long before you found out about it. You were the perfect patsy to do their dirty work."

"I know." Vivian leaned her head back against the swing, closing her eyes. "But still, I didn't have to be a part of it. I won't be a part of it anymore."

"What are your plans?" Lucas listened to the katydids sing out through the darkness. He looked over to where Vivian's head leaned back so close to his shoulder. "You aren't leaving Carson's Bayou, are you? I've kind of gotten used to you being around."

"I'm not sure." Vivian opened her eyes and rolled her head over, looking Lucas in the face. "I moved here to make a name for myself, build a solid reputation, be somebody that people would want to know." Her shoulders shrugged as her voice caught. "That's why I was doing all of this remodeling and buying. I was trying to make myself good enough. But then, it's like God was determined to show me I would never be good enough, no matter where I lived, or what I bought."

"Vivian." Lucas reached his arm out, easing it around her shoulders and drawing her close to his side. "None of us can ever be good enough on our own. We all have sin that has muddied us up. You go to church, you've read the Bible, you know that."

"My head knew it." Vivian's hand reached up and wiped a tear as it started to run down her cheek, "but I think my heart had forgotten about it until the other day—after I started to really think about who I was, and how I was starting off my life here." She leaned her head over and rested it on Lucas's shoulder. "Thank you for saying what you said about my father."

"I shouldn't have said it." Lucas rested his chin on the top of Vivian's head, drinking in the feel of how her shoulder fit perfectly under his arm. "I was mad at you because I wanted to come over here and save the day for you. I was sure you would tell me what a great guy I am." He stretched his eyes wide in the darkening light. "When I saw you here with Finley Parson, not really needing my help, it hurt my pride."

"No." Vivian swatted away another tear, her voice stronger with conviction. "No, what you said was right, and I needed to hear it. I was heading down the same path as my father. I imagine he started off with good intentions as well. His lifestyle and spending habits trapped him into doing things to make money that eventually led to him going to prison." She pulled her shoulders away from Lucas and twisted around so she could see his face. "I needed that punch in the gut to make me stop and think."

"Hmph." The corners of Lucas's lips flattened into a frown. "Some friend I am. Anyway, I'm glad it all worked out, even if I did act like a buffoon."

"Lucas." Vivian's voice grew soft as she tried to see his face. "I don't have a lot of friends like you do. I don't know what I need to do to be a friend like you are... and I'm sorry I let you down."

The coolness of the air hit his skin as Vivian stood from the swing, no longer at his side. "I only need you to do one thing," he whispered through the darkness as he watched her back disappear inside her front door. "I need you to stay."

The following morning, right as Lucas was finishing his coffee, Vivian surprised him by showing up on his doorsteps and inviting him on an early morning jog. Lucas had dressed and made the run, but on the way home, pulled into the gas station and bought them each two scoops of ice cream to reward all their hard work.

During their jog, Vivian explained that the realtor was coming over at eight that morning with the potential buyer.

"Would you mind hanging around for a while?" Vivian asked, climbing out of the old truck and slamming the door. "I know I live in the house, but let's face it, you know a whole lot more about Maw Cil's house than I ever will."

"Sure." Lucas followed Vivian across the street to her house, glancing down at his watch. "We should have a few minutes to talk before the realtor arrives."

Vivian opened the gate of her picket fence and they walked to the front porch, each with their ice cream cones in their hands. "I'm kind of anxious to see this guy that's buying the place. I hope he has a family. I know it doesn't really matter, but I would love for a family to live here with kids."

"That would be nice," Lucas said, looking around the yard, avoiding Vivian's gaze. "Listen, I made a phone call to Clay Carson. I went to school with him and his cousin, Blaze." Lucas paused and ran his tongue along the side of his waffle cone before the vanilla ice cream dripped down onto the porch steps of Maw Cil's house. "I want you to go with me to talk with him after while. I think he may be able to help us."

Vivian raked her lips across the top of her chocolate ice cream cone, forming a thin brown mustache on her upper lip. "Does he have a place where you might want to put the new shelter?" She ran her tongue across her upper lip, smearing the chocolate a little higher on her skin. "Thank you for being here when the realtor comes. I know you need to go in to work and not babysit me while I try to sell this house, but the sooner I sell, the sooner I can help with the new shelter."

"Here." Lucas leaned a little closer to Vivian where they sat, side by side, on the steps. He raked his thumb softly across the skin above her lip. "You have a little ice cream on your face." A bolt of lightning shot up his fingertips as Vivian reached up, holding his hand. He swallowed as she drew his thumb to her lips, kissing off the chocolate from his thumb.

"Thank you," Vivian whispered, releasing his hand and pulling in a deep breath. "When I love something... like ice cream... I can't stand to let it go to waste." Her eyes pulled away from his as another drip of chocolate ran down the cone and over her fingertips. "Oh man. We better hurry up and finish these. The realtor will be here in a minute with the man wanting to see the house." She raised the cone to her lips, licking the ice cream from her fingers and getting more on her face. "I need to at least look halfway presentable to whomever it is. I don't have time to change, but I don't want to be covered in ice cream."

Lucas felt his face growing warm, as his eyes drank in her lips, her face, her eyes. He scooted over on the steps just a hair, giving himself a little room to breathe. He needed to talk to her, explain a few things, and he was running out of time. The melted ice cream ran down his fingers and dripped onto the ground. "I think I'm done with this one."

"Hand it here." Vivian stood and took the cone from his hand, smiling down at him with another brown mustache. "I will toss these, and we can wash up before they get here."

"Uh, there's something I need to tell you." Lucas rose slowly, his tone causing Vivian to stop walking up the steps and turn.

"Is something wrong?" Vivian's eyes widened with concern as she took another lick of the chocolate ice cream, now running like a river down the cone and dripping on the top of her tennis shoe. "Have I stuck my foot in my mouth again?"

"No, it's not you. First of all, Clay Carson is a lawyer here in town. I told him about you and what happened with your current firm. He said his firm might want to hire you."

"Oh, Lucas!"

"Wait. That's not what I need to tell you." Lucas looked at Vivian's face as she watched his with trusting eyes. "Before I tell you this, I want you to know that I wasn't trying to sneak around behind your back. I just didn't know how to tell you."

"Lucas?" The smile on Vivian's face slipped away as she listened to his words. "What is it?"

"Well, I'm the guy that's coming over to look at your house. When I saw the For Sale sign in your yard the other day, I called and made the offer. I want you to stay and rent the place from me." Lucas stared at Vivian, waiting for her to respond.

Vivian looked at Lucas's face for a brief second before her eyes crinkled with a smile and her lips, along with the brown mustache, stretched into a wide grin. "I don't know what to say."

Vivian's arms wrapped around his shoulders as Lucas felt the cold ice cream cones squish against the back of his neck and head. He held her close, pressing his lips against hers as she tried to pull away, remembering the mess she had in her hands. As his lips found hers, and the longing in his embrace reacted with hers, Vivian melted against him. For a minute he forgot all about the house, the realtor appointment, even the ice cream she let drop down his back.

"Does this mean you are okay with me being your landlord for a while?" Lucas asked when he finally pulled away. "Will you stay in the house?"

"I don't know?" Vivian tilted her head to the side, smiling up into his face. "What will people think if they learn I am kissing my landlord?"

"They will think that your landlord has fallen for the little girl who used to come to town every summer and shamelessly bossed him around until she left again." The laughter in Lucas's eyes softened as he raised his hand up and touched her cheek, lowering his mouth to hers. "They will think that Lucas Wade is in love with Vivian Bradford."

"Will they be right?" Vivian whispered, tilting her face up to reach his lips.

"Perfectly right."

"Good." Vivian pulled her lips away and looked into Lucas's eyes. "Because Vivian Bradford is most definitely in love with Lucas Wade."

EPILOGUE

"*L*adies and gentlemen, please give a round of applause to Miss Vivian Bradford. Without her generosity and wanting to continue Cecille Bradford's tradition of helping others in Carson's Bayou, we would not be here today, celebrating the opening of the new Good Samaritan House."

Heat rose up Vivian's neck as the crowded room full of people all turned in her direction in one movement. She pushed her lips into a smile, trying to appear gracious. "I thought Mrs. Frances was not going to make a big deal about this," she said, never letting the smile slip as she looked around the dining room of the new Good Samaritan House, filled with supporters, donors and well-wishers of the community at the grand opening of the new shelter.

"Oh, she's not." Lucas reached over and took Vivian's hand, giving it a squeeze. "She wanted to have the TV station here with a big press release and get the mayor to make a speech. She really reined it in."

"Oh, good grief." Vivian finally blew out the breath she

was holding as Mrs. Frances went on to mention several other people who had worked on the new building, getting the Good Samaritan House built in record time. "How come she only said Wade Brothers Construction?" Vivian's brow puckered in a frown as she looked over at Lucas, dressed in his black suit, white shirt, and silver tie. "How come she didn't call out your name as one of the people working on all of this?"

"Let's just say we have an understanding." Lucas's brown eyes twinkled with laughter as they began to clap as Mrs. Frances's speech drew to a close. "Besides, look at you." Lucas let go of her hand and stepped back, admiring her red cocktail dress with lace and satin bodice, and full tulle skirt. The elegant fifties vibe of the dress showed off her figure in a classy way that he couldn't help but admire. "I want everybody here to know who you are, and that you are here with your fiancé."

Vivian's eyes lit up in a genuine smile as she looked down at the round solitaire diamond ring on her left hand. A warm fuzzy feeling tickled inside her as she thought about their wedding scheduled for next month. It wouldn't be an enormous affair, only the bride and groom, Langston, and Mrs. Albertson at the church. Lucas had offered to give her the wedding any girl would dream of, but Vivian declined, realizing that having a small, intimate wedding sooner, without all the fuss, would be a gift to both of them.

Vivian had started working with Clay Carson two weeks after Lucas bought the house. Lucas proposed on the day she paid him her first month's rent. Vivian had felt terrible about Lucas buying Maw Cil's house, thinking he had taken on a financial burden he could not afford so she would not lose her grandmother's family home. Finally, after the proposal, he put her mind at ease by letting her look at his financial holdings. The man that lived across the street in the three-bedroom ranch-style house and drove the beat up old pickup truck... the man who wore blue jeans and tee-shirts and spent his days off work building houses for the needy and volunteering at the local shelter was one of the wealthiest men in Louisiana.

Vivian looked up from the ring on her finger into Lucas's brown eyes. "Has anyone ever told you that you are a special man, Lucas Wade?"

The corners of Lucas's lips turned up in a slow, lopsided smile. "Well, not lately."

"Well, you are. Very special."

She's working hard for a better life
He's working hard to win her heart

Business Smarts & Reckless Hearts Carson's Bayou Series
Book 2

CHAPTER ONE

"*J*ust one more bite." Fiona held the spoon up to the old woman's pale, drooping lips. *Nana, are you even in there?* She looked into the faded blue eyes, void of emotion, or even recognition of who Fiona was or what she was doing. Fiona's heart tugged. Where was the woman who used to live in that body? "Nana." She touched the cool spoon to her grandmother's lips, coaxing her to take one more bite of the scrambled eggs. "Eat this, and I will bring you a Hershey kiss this afternoon."

Fiona dropped the spoon back onto the plastic tray. It was no use. Nana was done eating for now. She threw her thick braid of chestnut hair back over her shoulder and sighed. "It's okay," she whispered, leaning over and gently kissing her grandmother's wrinkled cheek. "It's not your fault. You're doing the best you can." Fiona pressed Nana's boney cheek against her own and blinked back tears. Not only had Nana forgotten the faces of the grandchildren she raised as her own, she had also forgotten how much she enjoyed eating. The skeletal figure in front of her was just a shadow of the plump, jovial woman who was once the rock Fiona and her two siblings had clung to after their mother abandoned them all those years ago.

Fiona took the adult sized bib from around her grand-mother's neck and glanced at the clock on the wall behind her. Ten minutes till seven. She would probably be late for work again, but she couldn't help it. Trina, the head nurse of the memory care section of the nursing home, assured Fiona that her grandmother ate twice as much for Fiona as she did for any of the nursing staff, no matter how much they tried to entice her. There was no way Fiona could make it to her grandmother's noon meal. She would be there for Nana's breakfast and dinner feedings every day. That was going to happen, no matter what. She tucked in a wayward curl that had already escaped her braid and blinked back a tear. Nana was fading away a little more every day right before her eyes.

"She ate seventy-five percent, Flo." Flo rolled the dolly over to where they sat, and Fiona handed the nursing assistant Nana's breakfast tray, tearing her eyes away from the woman who barely resembled the grandmother she loved. "I've got to run. Call if you need me."

Fiona hugged Nana's boney shoulders one more time. She stepped away from the wheelchair and hurried to the exit. Her nimble fingers punched in the passcode, keeping the Alzheimer's patients securely in the building. Snatching up a fold in her long gauzy skirt, she jogged across the parking lot to her little Volkswagen Beetle. She tossed her canvas bag in the passenger's seat and turned the key in the ignition. Fiona held her breath. The engine turned over and coughed to a start. *Thank you, Lord.* Sawyer, Fiona's brother, older by eleven months, was an ace mechanic. His willingness to tinker with her vehicle and scavenger used replacement parts as needed was the only reason she had a car that would run.

Fiona absolutely loathed the way their backyard looked like a junkyard, with old car parts scattered hither and yonder. There were always at least three vehicles in different stages of repair that she had to push the mower around.

She shouldn't complain, not really. Sawyer's side business of buying wrecked cars, fixing them, and reselling them, helped pay the bills. One day soon, he planned on opening his own auto body/mechanic shop, but he had to keep dipping into his savings to pay for things like a broken stove, or their little sister's trip to the dentist. No, her car needed fixing, but she would not bother Sawyer as long as it would get her from point A to point B.

The little car sputtered into the parking lot behind the coffee shop. She killed the engine, and the Beetle sighed, relieved it survived the trip. Fiona's gray eyes scanned the lot. *Oh, man.* Gary Denton's truck was already there. Gary, her boss, was aware she stopped by and fed her grandmother every morning, but until last week, he didn't know that she was sometimes ten or fifteen minutes late starting her shift.

Thank goodness for Sarah. She clocked Fiona in on days she was running late. Fiona always made sure she stayed an additional ten or fifteen minutes after clocking out in the afternoon, or worked through part of her lunch break, so she was not actually stealing the wages. That; however, didn't matter to Gary. He had dropped in last week at 7:00. She hadn't gotten there until 7:10, but was miraculously already clocked in. No one would tell Gary who had punched the time clock for her. He immediately put her on probation, along with the other two employees who refused to rat her out. Her behind was already on the line.

This day was not starting off well. Fiona pushed open the back door of Bayou Bean and stumbled through the doorway. She glanced down at the untied shoestring of her white Converse, then back to the time clock where Gary stood.

"Pete called in." Gary looked down over the top of his black horn-rimmed glasses sitting on the tip of his pointed nose. Even though his five foot nine inch frame was only two inches taller than Fiona, his icy stare always made her feel small. "I need you to help Sarah at the counter."

"Uh." Fiona glanced toward the time clock. "Yes, sir. Let me just clock in."

Gary stepped to the side and waved his hand in front of him. "By all means. Please do."

Fiona grabbed her card from the metal tray on the wall and quickly punched in. Gary turned and headed toward the tiny kitchen area where she preferred to work. She grabbed a dark brown canvas apron from the peg nearby and slipped it over her head. *Lord, you know I have to feed Nana, and I need this job. Please make Gary go light on me.* She tied the strings of her apron around her narrow waist and gave them an extra hard tug. It would take a miracle to keep Gary off her back today, that was for sure.

Fiona stepped into the front of the brightly lit coffee house. She inhaled the revitalizing aroma of freshly ground beans that appropriately filled the shop. The whirring of the espresso machine blended with the chatter of the customers in the busy, little shop.

Sarah looked over her shoulder and spied Fiona. A bright smile flashed on her face. Fiona hurried to the counter, a twinge of guilt stinging her gut. She forced a cheery smile in place and looked back at her friend. *Why did*

I ever put Sarah in this predicament? These are my problems, not hers.

"Gary has been breathing down our necks all morning," Sarah whispered, stepping up to where Fiona started taking the order from a blond-headed man in a tee-shirt and jeans.

The guy was a regular, so Fiona had already started ringing him up before he spoke. Sarah knew almost all the regulars by name. Of course, Sarah, being Sarah, had learned everything about everyone she ever met within the first five minutes of meeting them. Fiona was not shy, but she did not find it necessary to delve into the inner workings of the past of every person she encountered at Bayou Bean the way her friend did. Dealing with her own life occupied too many of her thoughts lately. She did know what most of the regulars ordered. Learning those tidbits of information made her life run a little smoother.

"He met me at the time clock." Fiona handed the man across the counter his receipt and turned to her friend. "Look, I am really sorry I got you involved in my mess." She looked at the room full of people sitting at the little tables sipping their drinks or standing in line waiting to be served. "You got slammed this morning."

"It's no problem." Sarah reached her arm around Fiona's shoulders and gave a quick squeeze. "It just got this way. I promise. Besides, you would do the same for me." Sarah looked behind her where Gary stood in the doorway, his lips squeezed together in a thin line. "We better get to hopping. The dragon is going to start breathing fire out his nose and light this place up if he sees us actually being nice to each other."

Fiona glanced over her shoulder at Gary, then tugged on the bottom of her pale pink tee-shirt. She could talk to Gary after the rush of customers slowed down. Her hours were 7:00 to 2:00, but if she explained her situation to him again, maybe he would let her come in at 7:30, or even 8:00, and work later. She pulled a deep breath in through her nose and turned back to the next customer. She had to figure something out. It wasn't fair to Sarah to keep making her work short-handed, even if she acted like it was no big deal.

ACKNOWLEDGMENTS

As always, I am thankful to the Lord for giving me this crazy brain that keeps spinning tales day and night for me to write. Please pray that I will be able to continue to grow in my ability to write believable Christian faith into my stories that will share the light of the Savior. I have been undeservedly blessed by the gift of faith and I want it to be seen in my stories, no matter what genre I stumble into.

Thank you to my husband who supports me as I continue to plod along and pursue this love of writing. I think one reason I like writing about heroes is because I live with one every day.

Thank you to my writer friends who pull me back up when I fall into a fit of gloom and think my words need to be stuffed in a drawer, unfit to be read by anyone. You have pulled me through once again.

A LITTLE ABOUT KC HART

KC Hart is the author of inspirational romance and humorous southern cozy mysteries with a Christian world view. KC lives in Mississippi with Mr. Wonderful, her husband of thirty-seven years, where she spends her days enjoying the grandkids, reading, writing, and playing her piano or guitar. One of her favorite things to do is sit on the back porch in the evening and eat watermelon before the mosquitos come out to play.

KC sincerely believes that well-written Christian fiction can change lives. When a novel has strong Christian principals woven intricately into a well-written plot, the reader bonds with lifelike characters who struggle with trials, temptations, and struggles that the reader identifies with. The reader identifies with these characters because she's been there. Everyone has fallen. That's why everyone needs a Savior.

Then, when these same characters turn to Christ the Savior to bring them through these dark moments, the reader finds hope. KC believes the story reminds the reader why she must lean on the Lord in her trying situations. Through the book's structure showing Christianity as the positive light for good that KC knows to be true, the reader also sees why she needs to be the hands and feet of Christ to others.

KC strives to show how the Lord uses situations, people,

and His Word to bring the lost to Him, and mold, prune and grow His children. She tackles challenging situations, powerful emotions, and spiritual warfare through engaging stories and true-to-life characters.

KC's favorite Bible verses are Philippians 2:5-8.

Sign up for KC's newsletter and receive a free eBook of Music Smarts and Humble Hearts

Business Smarts and Reckless Hearts

If you enjoyed this book, please take a few minutes to leave a review now. Authors, myself included, really appreciate this, and it helps draw more readers to books they may enjoy as well. Thanks! KC

Follow KC on her social media platforms

https://www.bookbub.com/profile/kc-hart?list=author_books

https://www.goodreads.com/author/show/20570083.K_C_Hart

BOOKS BY KC HART

.